BELLE'S BRIDLE

The Gateway series:

and other titles

BELLE'S BRIDLE

Beryl Bye

LUTTERWORTH PRESS
Guildford Surrey England

First published 1973
Reprinted 1981

Copyright © 1973 Lutterworth Press
All Rights Reserved

ISBN 0 7188 2019 3

PRINTED IN GREAT BRITAIN
BY MACKAYS OF CHATHAM LTD

CONTENTS

Chapter 1

THE NAME ON THE BROWBAND

IT all happened so quickly that afterwards, when the girls were discussing what had happened, no one was quite sure what had triggered things off. One moment the three of them were walking their ponies sedately along the country road leading towards the common, and the next Jane had been catapulted head-first into a yielding heap of gravel which was piled haphazardly by the roadside. Belinda and Cathy reined-in their startled horses and for a moment didn't know whether to be amused or concerned. Then, as Jane scrambled to her feet looking cross rather than in pain, the two of them could not disguise their grins.

"I'm glad you think it's funny," Jane said coldly, advancing upon her truant pony, who had cantered on a few steps and then stopped, looking speculatively back at her mistress.

Jane took a firmer grip upon her whip.

"Oh don't whack her, Jane," Cathy begged. "You haven't found out what frightened her yet."

"And what about her frightening me?" Jane wanted to know. "A fat lot she cared about that."

Belle, Jane's grey mare, seeing the menace in

her mistress's eye, started to back nervously as Jane advanced upon her.

"Wait," Jane commanded. The pony flicked her ears, torn between duty and common sense. "Come on, Belle, there's a good girl," Jane wheedled. "And I'll teach you to shy like that for nothing," she muttered under her breath.

"Jane, you mustn't hit her," Cathy begged again. "It wasn't just naughtiness. She was frightened of something. I wonder what it was?"

"If you give her a whacking it will only make her wary of being caught another time," Belinda pointed out sensibly. "Anyway it's too late now. She's probably completely forgotten what she's done."

Jane made a grab at Belle's bridle and, feeling her two friends' increasing disapproval, managed to control her anger, but she spoke to the pony sharply as she gathered the reins into her left hand and prepared to remount.

Cathy expelled her breath in a sigh of relief. She knew that Jane had a very quick temper and for a moment she had feared that Belle would get more than her just deserts.

"I wonder what did frighten her," Cathy persisted, turning her own bay pony, Kelpie, around, and carefully inspecting the road and the hedges. An old blue polythene sack that had once held fertiliser flapped gently in the light wind, half weighed down by gravel, and a crow flew squawking from a nearby tree, flapping its wings noisily, but neither of these things constituted a real source of terror to a normal well-behaved pony. There was a mechanical digger covered by a tarpaulin at the side of the road, awaiting a road workman's return, but the cover was tightly tied down and in no way looked menacing.

"It was probably a blade of grass," Jane said sarcastically. "Belle is the only pony I've known who can put on an act of being terrified by absolutely nothing."

"Oh come, that's a bit unfair," Belinda remonstrated. "She's normally ever so good. She didn't turn a hair when that motor-bike shot out of a turning yesterday, and even when that piece of corrugated tin blew off the roof of the barn last week she only flinched and threw up her head. It was us that nearly jumped out of our skins, if you remember."

"But sometimes she does seem to be frightened by things that the other ponies don't bother about," Cathy said thoughtfully. "And we never seem to be able to find out exactly what they are— or what it is," she corrected. "That is, if it's one particular thing. That reminds me," she went on, "I never did tell you the funny thing that I noticed about the browband on Belle's bridle. Here, get off a moment and I'll show you what I mean."

"You might have suggested it before," Jane said grumpily. "I've only just got on again."

Belinda and Cathy exchanged wry grins. It was obvious that Jane was in one of her moods and they would have to handle her with kid gloves until she got over it.

"It's about her name," Cathy said. "We've always called her Belle because that's what her last owner called her, and we've always presumed that it's spelt b-e-l-l-e like the French for beautiful."

"*Merci, Mademoiselle,*" Jane said. "I didn't know we were in for a French lesson."

"Oh shut up, Jane," Belinda said. "And let Cathy get on with it."

"Well, I was looking at Belle's bridle some months ago. The letters across the browband are nearly rubbed out—they were obviously only painted on in the first place—but you can just make out her proper name, and it wasn't Belle at all, it was Rebel and the b-e-l of her name is about all that's left. So her last owner must have got it wrong and thought it was l-e that was missing from the end and instead it was R-e missing from the beginning."

"Thank you, Detective Inspector Smith," Jane said. "But I can't see that your wonderful discovery helps us to understand why Belle—or Rebel, as you prefer to call her—shies at absolutely nothing with absolutely no warning, absolutely out of the blue."

"But don't you see," said Belinda, who was beginning to understand what Cathy was getting at, "perhaps Belle was called Rebel by her previous owners just because she does shy at nothing—or at what seems to be nothing to us," she corrected herself. "Perhaps they just decided that she was a nappy pony and gave her the name accordingly without ever bothering to find out the real trouble."

"I can remember the very first time you tried her," Cathy said thoughtfully. "I somehow sensed something wasn't quite right even then. I can remember your father asking me what I thought of her—and I couldn't exactly put my finger on anything but I had a vague feeling that she wasn't completely relaxed."

"So all we've got to do is to find out what she doesn't like," Jane said. "And what do you suggest we do then?" she asked Cathy.

"Well, I suppose we have to spend a lot of time and trouble re-educating her," Cathy said. "So that we can convince her that there's nothing to be afraid of."

"It could be snakes," Belinda said. "I've read somewhere that horses don't like snakes."

"And I shouldn't think they like lions either," Jane ridiculed. "But this isn't the African jungle, you know. You can't honestly say the place is alive with snakes."

Belinda blushed and looked a bit silly.

"But we do have grass snakes," Cathy defended her. "And slow-worms. I think it's a perfectly reasonable suggestion."

"Well, I don't," Jane said. "You can't tell me that there was a thumping great snake about to cross the road just then. It's not even as if we're going through a field."

"Well, what about sheep?" Cathy said. "There's a whole flock in the field over there."

"You might just as well say Belle's afraid of cows or pigs or chickens," Jane said. "For goodness' sake be sensible. The pony lives on a farm, doesn't she? And she sees all kinds of animals every day."

"It must be something," Cathy said stubbornly. "And I vote we try and find out what it is."

"We might have to trace back through her previous owners," Belinda reminded them. "I think that would be rather fun. We can compile a whole life story of all her owners and perhaps write a book about them—you know, like Black Beauty."

"Considering Belle is only five years old it isn't going to be a very long book," Jane said dryly. "But it might be interesting tracing back her owners all the same. I would like to find out what has made her so jumpy, and it would be quite a challenge trying to see if we could make her forget her fear.

"We'd have to start with Mr. Lance," she went on thoughtfully. "And then find out how long he had her and where he got her from. Of course we *could* discover that he bought her at a place the other end of England. If so it will make our enquiries far more difficult."

"Oh, don't let's cross bridges like that until we come to them," Cathy begged, "or we'll never get anywhere. Sufficient for the day is the evil thereof."

"What a funny thing to say," Belinda laughed. "What does it mean?"

"Oh, it comes out of the Bible," Cathy said. "Mummy is always using it. It means, just sort out the troubles that have got to be solved today and don't go worrying about what may happen tomorrow because half the time it doesn't happen anyway."

"Clear as mud," Jane commented. "Anyway sometimes you *have* to think ahead to things that are going to happen tomorrow. Like that Maths test, for instance. Ugh. I can't see Miss Bright being very pleased if I don't look ahead and do a bit of revision for it."

"It's great having both Miss Bright and Joy teaching at the school, isn't it?" said Cathy. "Although I have to remember ever so hard to call Joy Miss Wills." (Joy and she had been friends since first they met a couple of years before.)

"I wonder if she's still disappointed about having to come home from Africa because of the revolution," Belinda said, thinking, like Cathy, of those anxious days when Joy had had to break off her first missionary efforts and fly home to England. "Although she and Miss Bright seem ever so happy settled in their little cottage."

"I think Joy would be happy anywhere," Cathy said, "as long as she was sure she was where God wanted her to be. She told me once that that's the difficult part. Being absolutely sure that you're in the right place."

"But wouldn't she get a vision or something?" Jane suggested. "That's what happened to that man we were learning about at Bible Class. A kind of eerie voice came out of the air and told him to go out into the desert where that chap with the chariot was driving along wanting someone to explain the Bible to him."

"But that doesn't often happen today," Cathy pointed out. "You have to keep on praying to find out what God wants you to do and where He wants you to be. And you have to read the Bible and really listen, believing He will put a clear message into your mind so that you know what to do. It isn't always easy to be sure, Joy says, because our minds are so full of what we really want to do ourselves that it's quite easy to kid ourselves that our will is really God's will."

"Well, don't let's stand here all day," Jane said suddenly. "We were going for a canter up on the common, remember?"

As the girls were gathering up their reins, a pretty chestnut mare with a white blaze trotted up to a nearby gateway, and whinnied a greeting. Kelpie responded with enthusiasm, much to everyone's amusement!

"Isn't she gorgeous?" Cathy said. "I wonder who she belongs to?"

"Farmer Taylor probably," Jane suggested. "It's his land anyway."

"It looks as if she's in foal," Belinda remarked knowledgeably. "I'd love to have a mare in foal, wouldn't you?"

"You wouldn't be able to ride her much," Jane pointed out.

"I hadn't thought of that," Belinda admitted.

The three girls remounted and pressed their ponies forward into a smart trot, Belle striding on ahead with pricked ears and showing her best paces, as if to prove she was sorry for her previous misdeed.

Jane turned slightly in her saddle and critically watched Kelpie's neat trot.

"We really are jolly lucky," she called back to Cathy. "His leg is certainly one hundred per cent cured. There's not even the slightest hesitation in his movement."

"I don't know about 'lucky'," Belinda corrected justly. "It was care more than luck that did it. If Cathy hadn't nursed Kelpie so faithfully I'm sure his leg wouldn't have healed like it did."

Cathy patted Kelpie's rough neck with a gentle hand. Even now she couldn't really believe that the pony was truly hers. Jane's father, Major Parminter, had given him to Cathy when it wasn't certain if the pony would ever be completely sound again. But Cathy had nursed him devotedly and almost willed him to get better, and the little pony had responded to her love and care. Jane had wanted a bigger pony at the time of Kelpie's accident anyway, so she had warmly approved her father's generous gift.

"Sometimes I get a guilty conscience about having Kelpie all for myself," Cathy confessed. "I can still remember how I used to envy Belinda having Candy when I never dreamed that I would ever have a pony of my own."

"But I was a selfish pig about her," Belinda admitted. "It never used to dawn on me to ask you if you wanted a ride."

"But you didn't mean to be selfish," Cathy protested. "It was just that you didn't think about it. Even at gymkhanas and things it's easy not even to notice girls and boys who are just standing around and watching. It never occurs to us to ask any of them if they'd like to have a ride—even between events. I bet they'd jump at the chance if we did."

"But I'd feel silly," Jane objected. "Supposing they refused?"

"I bet they wouldn't," Belinda argued. "They must be mad about horses to take the trouble to come to a gymkhana—just to watch—knowing there won't be a chance of actually riding."

"I've wondered lately if we ought to try and do something useful with the ponies," Cathy said.

"Such as what?" Jane wanted to know.

"I don't know quite," Cathy admitted, skilfully holding the common gate open for Belinda and Candy to go through.

"You'd better pray about it," Jane said, half-jokingly, "and see what happens."

"What a good idea," Cathy said seriously, as she refastened the gate.

"Beat you to the coppice," Jane called, giving the eager Belle her head.

The girls raced three abreast across the short

heathery turf of the common, and the ponies lengthened their strides as the ground flashed away under their eager hooves. Kelpie's mane streamed in the wind as the smaller pony tried gamely to match his pace to that of the two rather bigger and stronger ponies who had drawn slightly away. Cathy put firm but gentle pressure upon the reins and spoke quietly to Kelpie whose ears flicked backwards at the sound of her voice.

"Steady, pony," Cathy said. "Let them go. They're bigger than you, and I know you would do your best to beat them if I wanted you to."

The pony slackened his stride obediently, and without a vestige of envy Cathy watched the other two fighting it out. For her it was enough to be riding her very own pony—and such a sweet pony too—on the wide open spaces of the common on a glorious day in April. She felt brimming over with happiness.

"Thank you lots, God." The prayer sprang silently to Cathy's lips. "Thank you lots for letting things work out so that I've got Kelpie for my very own. I didn't deserve it, God. I know that. And, God—if you want us to use our ponies in some way for you—by sharing them or something —please show us how to do it. Because I'd like to share Kelpie. To try to make someone else as happy as I am."

"I think I won by a short head," Jane claimed triumphantly as she and Belinda reined-in at the coppice and Cathy cantered up easily to join them. "What do you think, Cathy? You had a better chance to judge being behind."

"I wasn't noticing," Cathy had to confess. "I was thinking of something else."

"I think you did win, Jane," Belinda conceded peaceably, patting the sweating Candy's neck. "Belle can't half go when you let her out, can't she? I suppose we really ought to get used to calling her Rebel, though. If that's her name."

"She certainly is a Rebel," Jane said, giving the grey a friendly smack on the rump. "But I must say she can move when she wants to. It's just like flying.

"I've been thinking over what we were saying about letting other people ride the ponies sometimes," she went on suddenly.

"I shouldn't think you had time to think about anything during that mad race," Cathy laughed.

"Well, I did," Jane said. "And I was wondering. What do you think about lending them to some of the children from that special school just outside the village? That place that used to be Oakwood Manor, on the Trackley Road."

"Lending them?" Belinda said doubtfully. "Without us?"

"Of course not, silly," Jane said impatiently. "You don't think I'd trust anyone else with Rebel if I wasn't there to supervise? I meant offering to take the ponies there and let the kids have rides. Just up and down the drive or something."

Cathy was a bit indignant. She had prayed the prayer to God, and now here was God sending the answer to Jane. She didn't think it was really fair.

"But some of them have got irons on their legs," she said slowly. "It would be an awful responsibility."

"Nonsense," Jane said. "We wouldn't let them go on their own, of course. We'd keep a tight hold of the bridles all the time."

"We could ask," Belinda said doubtfully. "I think there's a matron or someone in charge. But I don't know that they would be very keen on the idea. They might not trust us."

"Of course they would trust us," Jane insisted. "I expect they'd be jolly grateful to us for suggesting it. They ought to be anyway."

"We'd better walk the ponies back," Cathy said. "They're pretty hot after that gallop."

The other two nodded. "And we'd better go another way home just in case that dangerous great snake is still around!" Jane teased Belinda.

They rode gently back together towards the Parminters' farm. Belinda was living there too at the moment, for her parents were overseas in Hong Kong, and would be there for almost another two years. Cathy wondered how badly Belinda missed them. Jane's father and step-mother were very good to her, of course, and she went out to Hong Kong in the holidays, and Jane and she had become close friends: all the same, thought Cathy, it wasn't like living in your own home with your own parents.

She found herself remembering how sad she had been when first Belinda had moved into Jane's home. She had been afraid that now Belinda and Jane had each other, they wouldn't need her any longer. But it hadn't worked out like that at all. The three of them were all friends together: Jane with Belle, Belinda with Candy, and Cathy herself with her darling Kelpie. She bent forward to pat his neck and hummed to herself as she rode along after the other two.

Chapter 2

THE SEARCH CONTINUES

IT was Break, and Cathy and Belinda had volunteered to put out the materials for the Art Lesson which followed.

"I can't make out what is the matter with Jane," Cathy said, as she rinsed out the paint pots and filled them with clean water.

"Hasn't she told you?" Belinda said, surprised.

"Told me what?" Cathy wanted to know.

Belinda looked uncomfortable. "Well, I don't know that it's exactly a secret," she hedged. "But maybe she will want to tell you herself. She might be mad if I told you first."

Cathy was intrigued, but a little worried. She hoped it didn't mean that Jane was moving away, or something horrid like that.

"She's not moving, is she?" she asked sharply.

"No, of course not," Belinda said. "It's nothing like that."

"Then what is it?" Cathy demanded. "Is she going to have another horse, perhaps? I'm not sure she's all that happy with Rebel."

"That's just where you're wrong," Belinda said, rather glad to change the subject. "She *is* happy with Rebel. In fact, she's even more happy now that she thinks there may be some mystery associated with her and she's determined to find out what frightens her."

"Has Rebel played up lately?" Cathy asked with interest.

"Only once," Belinda said. "When we were stabling the horses at Mr. Styles's the other day."

"And what was the cause?" Cathy asked eagerly. "We really ought to write down all the circumstances each time she has one of her 'turns' —then, sooner or later, surely we should find a common denominator."

"You've got Maths on the brain," Belinda giggled. "Miss Bright would be proud of you."

"No, but seriously," Cathy said. "Tell me everything. Where you were, what was around at the time and exactly how it happened."

"We were just going through the stable gate," Belinda said. "The big five-barred one that leads to the yard."

"Perhaps it's gates," Cathy said. "Perhaps someone let one go on her once."

Belinda shook her head. "Impossible," she said. "Just think of all the gates we go through when we're out riding. She never turns a hair."

"What else?" Cathy demanded.

"There was a big van parked outside. One of those that carry animals. But that didn't cause it —it was stationary," she cut in before Cathy could interrupt. "Mr. Styles was forking hay down from the loft and his man was helping the van driver load some stock into the van."

"What stock?" Cathy asked. "Horses?"

"I don't think so," Belinda said. "I didn't notice particularly. You know Mr. Styles runs a kind of smallholding. There's always various animals around."

"But it wasn't snakes?" Cathy asked wickedly.

"No," Belinda agreed with a grin. "It wasn't snakes."

"Was it sheep?" Cathy asked.

"I don't think so," Belinda said. "I don't think he keeps sheep. And anyway," she reminded Cathy, "as Jane said the other day, Rebel can't possibly be scared of animals—she sees too many of them. There were chickens around. Just pecking and talking to themselves. And there was a tractor in the yard. I think Mr. Styles had used it to bring in some hay on the trailer."

"There was that tractor thing by the road when she shied last time," Cathy said quickly.

"That was a mechanical digger," Belinda said. "And anyway, she's not the slightest bit afraid of traffic, even when it's making a noise."

"Was Mr. Styles smoking?" Cathy asked.

"I can't really remember," Belinda admitted.

"I was wondering about fire," Cathy said. "Some horses are afraid of fire."

"But we weren't smoking the other day," Belinda laughingly pointed out. "It's got to be something that happened both times."

"Anyway perhaps we'll pick up a clue on Saturday when we go and see Mr. Lance," Cathy said. "Meanwhile we must watch Rebel carefully, and note absolutely everything that is around when she has one of her 'turns'."

"You make her sound like an old lady with a weak heart," Belinda giggled, "instead of a spirited five-year-old grey."

It wasn't until the following Saturday, when the girls were on their way to see Mr. Lance, that Cathy had the opportunity of asking Jane about the mystery that Belinda had only hinted at the week before.

"I say, Jane," she started, "Belinda had me worried the other day. I thought you were going to move. I should hate that."

"Move?" Jane said. "Of course we're not going to move. We've always lived here, ever since I was a baby. And Mummy and Daddy lived here too, before I was born."

Jane went very quiet and so did the other girls. Jane still didn't find it easy to talk about her real mother, who had died when she was quite a little girl. She had learned to accept the new Mrs. Parminter fairly naturally now, but Belinda and Cathy knew that it couldn't be quite the same as having a real mother of your very own.

"Have I told you about the baby?"

Jane's statement was so abrupt that Cathy wondered if she had heard aright.

"The baby?" she gasped. "Whose baby?"

"Miss Beckford's baby," Jane said coolly. "And Daddy's, I suppose."

Cathy didn't know what to say. Miss Beckford had been Jane's governess until she married

Jane's father, Major Parminter. (Belinda had gone on a little ahead, to leave the other two alone for a bit.)

"But she's not Miss Beckford now," Cathy said gently. "She's—well, Mrs. Parminter. Isn't it rather horrid to speak of her like that? With the baby coming, I mean."

"Is it?" Jane said coldly. "I never really thought of it."

"But aren't you pleased?" Cathy asked. "About the baby?"

"Pleased?" Jane said. "Why on earth should I be pleased? It's nothing to do with me after all."

"But won't it be fun to have a little brother or sister?" Cathy's face lit up at the thought. "I've always wished I'd had one."

"I can't say that babies have ever appealed to me much," Jane said, lifting one shoulder in a gesture of distate. "They're always crying, or dribbling, or wetting their nappies, it seems to me."

"Your father and step-mother must be awfully pleased about the baby," Cathy said. "When will it come?"

"I haven't bothered to enquire," Jane said. "You'd better ask them if you're so interested." Her tone made it perfectly clear that she didn't want to talk about the baby any more.

Rebel pricked up her ears as they approached the Lances' Farm.

"I wonder if she remembers?" Belinda said.

Mr. Lance was hosing down the yard when they

arrived. He didn't recognize them at first, but he recognized the grey mare. Then his eyes flicked to Jane's face in sudden remembrance.

"I thought it was my mare," he called, "How is she going?"

"Very well," Jane said. "At least most of the time," she corrected herself. "That's what I wanted to have a talk to you about."

A kind of veiled expression came over the man's face, but he moved over to the tap to turn off the water and wiped his hands on the seat of his corduroy trousers.

"She hasn't been playing up, has she?" he asked warily.

"Only sometimes," Jane said. "And we're trying to find out why. All of a sudden she goes jumpy and we never know when it's going to happen or what sets it off. We thought if we could find out what it is that frightens her we might be able to do something about it."

"Hasn't had you off, has she?" Mr. Lance asked uneasily.

"Once or twice," Jane admitted. "But it's not that that worries me—it's just that I want to know why."

Mr. Lance seemed relieved that Jane hadn't come to complain about the bad habits of the grey mare and his face relaxed a little.

"Well, to be honest with you, I don't know what it is that frightens her," he admitted. "She was just the same when I had her. But I could see that you were a good little rider with some experience so I reckoned that you wouldn't come to much harm. She had my little girl off a couple of times you see, and it made the child nervous. She got so that she wouldn't ride Belle any more."

"Rebel," Belinda said. "That's her real name. Didn't you know?"

"No," Mr. Lance denied. "She came to me as Belle and that's all we ever called her."

"It's on her bridle," Cathy said. "Ever so faintly, but it's there all the same."

"Did you ever notice what it was that frightened her in particular?" Jane asked.

Mr. Lance shook his head. "It wasn't traffic," he said positively. "I know that. She was just as likely to 'set off' if you were riding her across country."

Jane agreed. "That's what we've noticed."

"Where did you get her from?" Belinda asked.

"I bought her at the market," Mr. Lance said. "She came from a riding school. That's why I was surprised she wasn't better behaved."

"What riding school?" Jane pressed.

"Wendover," Mr. Lance said vaguely. "About eight miles away. You could easily enquire."

"I expect the address would be in the telephone directory," Belinda said. "Anyway we haven't got time to go there today."

The three ponies stood easily, half-asleep in the drowsy sunshine. It was very quiet on the farm. There were only familiar farm sounds of chickens clucking quietly to themselves and the movement of animals' feet over deeply littered stalls. From the farmhouse came the sharp snap of someone shaking rugs from a window, and the drone of a washing machine filtered out from somewhere deep within the house. Pigs snorted in the nearby sty and a dog barked. Only the ponies' ears registered the sounds, flicking backwards and forwards and showing that they were more awake than they appeared to be.

"Well," Jane said, "there doesn't seem to be anything more we can learn today. But thank you for stopping to talk to us all the same," she said, remembering her manners.

"You're welcome," Mr. Lance said. "And good luck with your search," he called as they turned their ponies and prepared to move off.

"We'll go to Wendover next week," Jane decided without consulting the others, who exchanged a grin at Jane's easy disposal of their free time.

"Let's take a picnic," Cathy suggested. "We can make it a nice day out."

"Good idea," Belinda said, and Jane nodded.

That evening Cathy decided to go and see Joy, who was living with Miss Bright in their new little cottage.

"You *have* made it nice," she said admiringly as she followed Joy into the pretty sitting-room.

"I must say we're pleased with it," Joy agreed. "It's our first attempt at decorating."

"You've got distemper in your hair," Cathy

giggled. "It looks as if you've gone in for streaking it. It's all the fashion."

"How awful!" Joy laughed, peering in the mirror at herself.

Miss Bright came through from the little kitchen carrying a tray of tea and biscuits. "What have you been doing with yourself all day, Cathy?" she wanted to know as the three of them settled down for a cosy chat.

"We've been out on the ponies," Cathy said. And she told her friends about the puzzle of Belle's bridle and how the three of them were embarking upon a voyage of discovery to try and find out the cause of the pony's fright.

"It's like a mystery book," Miss Bright said. "Do keep us in touch with how you get on."

"We've not got very far yet," Cathy admitted. "Mr. Lance—Rebel's previous owner—admitted that she was just as jumpy when they had her, and that's why they got rid of her. He seemed relieved that we hadn't come to complain. Apparently Rebel had his little girl off several times, and in the end she wouldn't ride her."

"Naughty of him not to have warned you about it before you bought the pony," Joy said.

"It was really," Cathy agreed. "He said he'd bought Rebel in the market, and that she was sold by a Wendover riding school. That's going to be our next target."

"Once Jane has got her teeth into this there'll be no stopping her," Sue Bright laughed.

"I know," Cathy said. Thinking about Jane

made her thoughtful. "She's not very happy at the moment, you know," she said suddenly.

"Jane?" Joy asked.

"Yes," Cathy said. "Did you know that Major and Mrs. Parminter are going to have a baby?"

"I did hear something of the kind," Sue Bright admitted.

"Jane's not not very pleased about it," Cathy said.

"I don't suppose she is," Joy remarked. "Things will be a bit different for her from now on."

"How do you mean?" Cathy asked.

"Well, Jane has always been the most important person at the farm," Joy pointed out. "It won't be easy for her to take second place."

"I thought she'd be pleased about the baby," Cathy said. "I would."

"I think you would be," Sue agreed. "But there would still be times when you would find it terribly hard not to be jealous."

"Is Jane jealous?" Cathy asked.

"I'm afraid so," Sue said. "That's why she can't be pleased about the baby coming."

"Jealousy is a horrid thing," Joy said. "The trouble is that the only person you really hurt when you're jealous is yourself. You try and hit out at other people, but you are the one who gets hurt the most."

"It gnaws away inside," Sue said. "Like an aching tooth that you won't have taken out."

"*Can* you have it 'taken out'?" Cathy asked.

"Only by the Lord Jesus Christ," Sue said.

"And even then it's quite painful—because every time you feel a twinge of the old gnaw, you've got to be pretty quick off the mark to ask him to deal with it."

"Saul was jealous, wasn't he?" Cathy said suddenly. "It's funny, we're doing him at Bible Class at the moment."

"Yes, and look what it did to him," Joy said. "It turned him from a strong, brave, popular, soldier king, to an embittered, half-mad, vicious man and all because he was afraid that the people might come to like David better than they liked him."

"Jane will have to be careful," Cathy said slowly. "Won't she?"

"Very careful," Sue agreed.

"And we will have to be very prayerful—on Jane's behalf," Joy suggested.

Chapter 3

JOY HAS SOME GOOD NEWS AND
JANE IS ANNOYED

ONE morning Joy had a rather important letter. It had a London postmark and she was curious to see who it was from. She opened it and sat reading it while she and Sue Bright were drinking their final cup of breakfast coffee before getting ready to go to school.

"Listen to this, Sue," she said. "It's from my uncle's solicitors. Apparently he's left nearly the whole of his estate to me."

"His estate?" Sue asked.

"Well, that's just the legal term meaning his money," Joy explained. "I never dreamed that he had done anything like that."

"Were you his next-of-kin?" Sue asked.

"No . . . Well, yes, perhaps I was," Joy said thoughtfully. "His older sister died some years ago, and my father was his only brother."

"How much is it?" Sue asked curiously. "Is it a lot?"

"It seems a lot to me," Joy admitted. "It's about fifteen thousand pounds. Actually I can't really take it in."

"Your bank manager won't be able to take it in either!" Sue said.

"Poor Uncle," Joy said slowly. "He was awfully sweet to me. Especially after Mummy and Daddy died. It was so senseless him being killed like that—by a stray bullet that wasn't intended for anyone in particular. He was so good and kind, Sue, and everyone loved him."

Sue put her hand lightly on her friend's shoulder. "It's no good still grieving, Joy," she said. "Nothing you can do can bring him back again. Not to this earth anyway."

"I know," Joy said. "But I still miss him, even so."

"What are you going to do with the money?" Sue asked, hoping to bring her friend into a more cheerful frame of mind.

"I haven't the slightest idea," Joy admitted. "It's all come as such a surprise. I thought Uncle might leave me something, of course, but it never entered my head that he had so much to leave anyway."

"It's an awful responsibility," Sue said slowly. "Like the story of the talents somehow. The more money you've got, the greater your responsibility to use it wisely."

"I'm sure God will show me how He wants me to use it," Joy said. "I shall ask Him anyway. What would you do with it if you were me?" she asked her friend seriously.

"I should buy a Christian Riding Centre," Sue said without hesitation.

"Would you really?" Joy said. "That's not a bad idea. Not that my riding would get me very

3

far at any Centre! It's as much as I can do to stay in the saddle at the moment!"

Sue laughed. "That's only because you haven't done much," she said. "You'd soon learn if you set your mind on it."

"Do you mean a residential Centre?" Joy wanted to know, still thinking about Sue's idea.

"Yes," Sue said. "You'd need a pretty big house and stables attached. Then you'd run courses—week-ends in term-time, and whole weeks in the holidays—and in the mornings and evenings you'd have really good sessions of Christian teaching, so that the holiday was a physical one and a spiritual one as well—both at once."

"It would be a big venture," Joy said doubtfully.

"But very exciting," Sue insisted. "And it could be wonderfully used by God really to build young people up in the Christian faith." She looked at her watch. "Help, it's twenty to nine. We'd better nip round pretty quickly and get on our way."

Jane, Belinda and Cathy had agreed to meet after school and go to see the Matron in charge of the Children's Home about Jane's idea of teaching some of the children to ride.

"I'm still not sure it's a very good idea," Cathy said doubtfully as they shouldered their satchels at four o'clock.

"It's only because you didn't think of it," Jane said rather nastily as they walked along.

"That's horrid," Belinda said shortly.

"Perhaps it's a bit true," Cathy was forced to admit.

The Matron seemed very surprised to see the three young girls standing on the doorstep when she answered their ring some ten minutes later.

"Good afternoon," she said. "What can I do for you?"

"Well, it's like this," Jane began. "We've all got ponies, you see, and we like riding very much. We were talking about it the other day and decided perhaps we ought to use our ponies to help somebody else. So that they could get some fun out of them as well, you see. So we thought about the children in your Home, and decided that it would be a good idea to give some of them riding lessons. We thought it would make a nice change for them. We're very experienced and responsible," she added, sounding very much like her father.

Belinda wished that Jane hadn't got a smear of green paint across one cheek and that they hadn't used the elastic band from one of her plaits for flicking paper pellets across the room at that objectionable Mary Witter. Then Jane might have looked a bit more "experienced and responsible". She was very conscious of her own school socks nestling in rings around her ankles, and Cathy's ink-daubed fingers and bursting blazer pockets. They would have made a much better

impression if they had been neatly dressed in riding clothes and had, perhaps, brought their
ponies with them.

The Matron was looking them up and down
and Belinda had a shrewd suspicion that she was
thinking much the same.

"Well, it's very kind of you to think of the
children," the Matron said at last. "But we do
have to be terribly careful with them, you know.
Especially the ones that have to wear appliances
on their legs."

"Oh, we'd be frightfully careful," Jane assured
her. "We weren't thinking of letting them go out
on their own."

"I realize that," the Matron said. "But I still
feel it would be too much responsibility for you.
Now if you were older perhaps, or there was an
adult in charge . . ." She left the sentence
unfinished.

Jane was getting a bit fed up. It had never
dawned on her that their generous offer might be
refused.

"But we're perfectly responsible," she said
indignantly. "We're all members of the Pony
Club and we've been riding for years."

"I'm not doubting that you're very competent
riders yourselves," the Matron said soothingly.
"But that's not quite the same as being responsible for a number of disabled small children who
have never been on a horse before. I'm very
touched at your kind thought but I'm afraid—for
the safety of the children—that I don't feel that I

can accept it. Perhaps if your parents were prepared to supervise it might be possible to arrange
something," she suggested pleasantly. "And now
you'll have to excuse me. The children will be
coming in for their tea."

"What a cheek!" Jane burst out as soon as they
were out of earshot down the drive.

"Well, I suppose she's got to consider the safety
of the children," Belinda said slowly. "And you
must agree we don't look madly responsible and
efficient and grown-up at the moment."

"Nor would she if she'd been slaving at school
all day like we have," Jane snorted.

"It might have been better if we'd changed
first," Belinda suggested. "And called with the
ponies on the way back home."

"Then Cathy couldn't have come," Jane
pointed out.

"I can see what Belinda means though," Cathy
agreed. "We do look a bit of a wreck."

"I think she ought to have been jolly grateful,"
Jane said with feeling. "Fancy turning down an
offer of free rides for the children without even a
'Thank you'."

"She did say it was a kind thought."

"Well it's the last time I'm having any kind
thoughts," Jane said rather sweepingly. "So
much for your good ideas about sharing the
ponies," she said, turning on Cathy. "And it was
a fat lot of good you praying about it."

"I hardly had time to pray before you came up

with the answer," Cathy reminded her promptly. "The first thing that comes into one's mind isn't always the right answer, even though it may seem like it. Perhaps we ought to wait a bit and see what turns up."

"Well, I'm going home," Jane said. "I'm fed up with the whole business. See you tomorrow, Cathy."

"Are we still going to Wendover on Saturday?" Cathy wanted to know.

"If it doesn't pour with rain," Jane said. "Which it probably will." She was feeling rather bad-tempered and didn't attempt to hide it.

Belinda and she were trotting along the flat stretch of road which led to Aggs Hill with their satchels bumping gently on their backs, when suddenly Rebel snorted, threw up her head, laid back her ears, and fought madly against Jane's restraining hands and legs.

"Look out, she's off again," Belinda warned, shortening Candy's reins in case of trouble. Rebel danced along, snorting down her nostrils and fighting every inch of the way, while Jane struggled to control the frightened pony.

"Whatever is it?" Belinda questioned, trying to identify the cause of the pony's fright. But Jane was too busy to answer.

It was the day for the refuse collection on Aggs Hill, and there were several dustbins placed on the grass verge ready for emptying, but Rebel didn't seem to be paying any particular attention to them. Belinda could see freshly dug furrows through a half-opened gate and lines of binder cord stretched between them with pieces of polythene attached for scaring off the birds. On the other side of the lane the field was muddy and the ground rooted up as if by pigs—or perhaps by cows milling at the gate whilst waiting to be milked. The clattering and clanging of pails and churns came from the open door of a farm outbuilding where the milk was being strained and churned. A jeep was coming down the road from the opposite direction but it pulled into the side when it saw Jane trying to bring her terrified pony under control. Now Rebel changed her tactics and instead of straining back on her haunches to avoid going forward, she came up into her bridle and behaved as if a ferocious beast was pursuing her from the rear. Jane held her with wrists of steel, and gradually the powerful surging muscles of the strong little pony relaxed and the wildness of her eyes became less pronounced.

Belinda drew level with Jane.

"You held her," she said admiringly.

"Only just," Jane admitted breathlessly, rather red in the face. "And look, she's in quite a lather. She is a little idiot the way she suddenly gets frightened at nothing."

"I wondered about the dustbins," Belinda said doubtfully. "But she didn't seem to be edging directly away from them."

"She wasn't," Jane said. "It was a sort of general terror—almost as if she smelled something in the air rather than shying at one particular thing."

"Thunder?" Belinda wondered.

"I didn't hear any, did you?" Jane said.

Belinda shook her head.

"What was in the fields each side of the lane?" Jane asked.

"I don't know," Belinda admitted. "One side was sown, I think—the other, cows or pigs— nothing terrifying."

"It really is a mystery," Jane said. "Look, she's as quiet as a lamb now. It's hard to believe she's the same pony."

"But it's jolly awkward," Belinda said. "One never knows what will set her off."

"We'll find out in the end," Jane said confidently.

She told her father about the pony's strange fits of terror while the girls were sitting in the pleasant farm kitchen doing their homework that evening. Major Parminter was interested but a little concerned.

"You're not nervous of her, are you, Jane?" he asked. "If so we'll get rid of her and get something else. I don't want you to have another fall."

"No, I'm not nervous of her," Jane reassured her father. "But I shall be glad when we have found out what scares her, because you can never quite trust her."

"Horses are strange creatures," Major Parminter said thoughtfully. "If something makes a really big impression on them when they're young, it's very difficult to make them forget it. I wonder who broke her? Some people are a bit unscrupulous in their methods. I once heard of a man who rode spirited young horses round and round a muck heap, on and on until they were absolutely exhausted, and their spirits were broken as well as their hearts."

"How absolutely awful," Belinda said. "Why aren't people like that sent to prison?"

"You've got to catch them at it," Major Parminter pointed out. "And that's easier said than done."

"There's a muck heap by Mr. Styles's gate," Belinda said thoughtfully. "Do you remember Rebel trying to bolt from there just after you had her? She skinned your leg on the gate on the way through."

"There's muck heaps everywhere," Jane pointed out. "Even in our own yard, and the only notice that Rebel has taken of *that* one is to trample through it and get her legs messed up just when I've spent half an hour making her look really decent." She turned to her stepmother. "Can we take a packed lunch on Saturday? We want to go to Wendover and see if we can trace the riding school where Mr. Lance bought Rebel before he sold her to us."

"Yes, of course," Mrs. Parminter answered. "Only don't be back too late, will you? I'd like you to come into the town with me and help me choose the pram. Perhaps Belinda would like to come too. We'll have tea at that nice place in the

High Street, and afterwards we'll buy you that new sweater you are needing."

"I hate shopping," Jane said. "And I don't know anything about prams. Have I *got* to go down to the town with you on Saturday?"

"I think it would be rather fun," Belinda put in quickly, seeing Mrs. Parminter was looking rather disappointed. "And we can go to Wendover quite early in the day. It won't take more than a couple of hours at the most."

"Of course if you don't want to come I wouldn't dream of forcing you," Mrs. Parminter said quietly to Jane. "I just thought it would be nice to have some company, that's all."

"Oh I'll come if you want me to," Jane said ungraciously. "But I'm not trailing round the shops for the whole of the afternoon."

"You really are horrid to Mrs. Parminter," Belinda said frankly to Jane as the girls were getting ready for bed. "She tries to be specially nice to you and you just snap her head off in return. You were never like it when she was your governess."

"Well, she *will* try and make me take an interest in her wretched baby," Jane said bitterly. "Surely she can see I just don't care about it?"

There was a pause.

"We're not much good, are we?" Belinda said at last. "Both of us have asked the Lord Jesus Christ to make us His children and we promised to try and live the way He wanted us to. But we don't do much about it."

"What should we do?" Jane demanded sulkily.

There was another long pause.

"Well—read our Bibles for one thing, I suppose," Belinda suggested. "Joy and Miss Bright always say that's the way God speaks to you and helps you."

Jane sighed and picked up her Bible from the table by her bed where it was half-hidden under a tin of saddle soap, a list of Pony Club fixtures, and a bag of rather ancient fruit drops which were stuck into a solid lump.

The Bible notes slid out from the pages.

"Where are we meant to be reading from?" Belinda asked, picking up her own Bible. "We haven't read them for ages."

"1 Samuel, Chapter 18, verses 6–16," Jane said, glancing down the passage.

"Belinda!" she exclaimed indignantly. "I believe you've done it on purpose."

Belinda looked up innocently. "Done what?"

"Made me start reading my notes tonight. Just tonight of all times. Listen to this. *Saul was furious and the words rankled*—What does rankled mean, anyway?"

Belinda picked up her school dictionary, which happened to be handy. "Festered," she read. "To go on hurting deeply."

"*—and the words rankled,*" Jane went on. "*They have given David tens of thousands and me only thousands; what more can they do but make him king?*

From that day forward Saul kept a jealous eye on David . . . And you can't tell me you didn't know it was that," Jane went on, all in the same tone of voice.

"I didn't know," Belinda laughed. "Honestly I didn't. Joy would say that's the way God is speaking to you."

But Jane had gone on reading.

"Wow!" she said at last. "Saul chucked a spear at David, to pin him to the wall—but he missed—twice." She paused thoughtfully. "At least I don't throw spears at my stepmother," she justified herself to Belinda. "Do I?"

"Sometimes words can hurt as much as actual blows," Belinda pointed out.

Jane didn't say any more, and neither did Belinda, but when Jane's stepmother came to say goodnight to the girls a few minutes later she was very surprised and pleased when Jane reached up her arms and pulled down her head to give her a quick but warm kiss.

Belinda noticed what had happened, although she quickly turned her head the other way and pretended not to.

Chapter 4

THE VISIT TO WENDOVER STABLES

" ARE you still praying that God will show us how to use our ponies for other people?" Jane asked Cathy suddenly, as they were on their way to Wendover the following Saturday morning.

"When I remember," Cathy said honestly.

"Well, I'm not," Jane said firmly. "I still can't get over that wretched Matron turning down our offer."

"But you can't make up your mind that the very first thing that comes into your head is the right thing, and if that doesn't work out you won't ask God for any further advice."

"Who can't?" Jane wanted to know.

"Well, you shouldn't then."

"I'm fed up with you two getting on to me," Jane said. "First it was Belinda and now you."

"I'm not getting on to you," Cathy denied.

"And I wasn't either," Belinda insisted. "It was just that we decided to start reading our Bibles again the other night, and Jane found a bit that was just like her. And she thought I'd known about it beforehand, and suggested reading it just because of what it said."

"About Saul and David?" Cathy asked.

"Yes, how did you know?" Jane demanded.

"We do have ·the same Bible Notes," Cathy pointed out.

"Anyway I didn't know what was in them," Belinda denied. "It just happpened, that's all."

"God probably made it happen," Cathy suggested.

"Well it was jolly funny, anyway," Jane said. "I wonder if we shall get anywhere today?" she went on. "Daddy said this Wendover place is very easy to find."

"Rebel is going nicely today," Belinda said. The grey was trotting in a beautifully collected manner with her head up and her ears pricked. "She's in superb condition."

"Daddy says she jolly well ought to be," Jane remarked. "Considering what it costs to keep her."

"I'm glad they all get on so well," Cathy said, gesturing to the ponies. "I expect Kelpie misses Rebel and Candy during schooldays though. Still, never mind—it will soon be the holidays, then they won't get split up."

"Riding to school does keep them in condition," Jane remarked. "They need much more exercise than Kelpie does, and they'd never get it during term-time if we didn't have that double journey to do. There just isn't time. It's lucky we've got Styles' Stable to leave them at all day."

"Mr. Styles has seemed worried lately," Cathy said. "Have you noticed?"

"Not particularly," Jane said. "What's he worried about?"

"I don't really know," Cathy confessed. "But I sometimes wonder if he finds the stables a bit much now he's getting older. He used to have that girl groom working full time but she's got another job now and he really has to rely on just casual help. He's got eight horses to look after. It's quite a lot for him."

"Major Parminter was reading a bit out of the local paper about the new motorway," Belinda said. "Apparently there are plans for taking part of it right through Bedborough."

"They couldn't do that," Jane said. "They wouldn't be allowed to."

"They *are* allowed to," Cathy said. "You often hear of people who have to move out of their houses because a new road is being built or something."

"I wouldn't move out," Jane said. "They could jolly well build their old road as close as they liked. I'd lock myself in with lots of food and cokes and things and aim a gun from an upstairs window. I'd like to see them try to turn me out of my very own house."

"People try that," Cathy said. "But they always move in the end. You would too."

"I wouldn't," Jane said, sticking her chin out fiercely. "Anyway, what's all this got to do with Mr. Styles?"

"Nothing really," Belinda admitted. "Only that part of the motorway would run very near to

Mr. Styles's stables. I wondered if that might be what's worrying him."

"I can't think why he lives on in that great big old house all by himself," Jane said. "It's absolutely massive. He only lives in two rooms at the most. The rest must be going to rack and ruin."

"Mummy and Dad have known him for years," Cathy said. "He's got a brother, you see, and they quarrelled. It was all a very long time ago."

"Then why don't they make it up?" Jane said. "It's silly to have a quarrel that goes on for years. I expect they've quite forgotten what they quarrelled about anyway."

"He doesn't live in Bedborough," Cathy explained. "The brother, I mean. So I don't suppose they ever see each other."

"Just because he's quarrelled with his brother, I don't see why he's got to live in that great big house on his own," Jane argued. "It's got nothing to do with it. It might be a good thing if the motorway *did* go near his stables. Perhaps it would make him move."

"But it would be horrid," Cathy said quickly. "And what about the children who ride at the stables? They're not all lucky enough to have ponies like us. They'd miss it dreadfully."

"Miss Bright would miss it too," Belinda said. "I saw her taking Joy out for a lesson the other day. Joy's getting quite good."

"She said she was jolly stiff afterwards," Jane

laughed. "She said she felt as if she wouldn't be able to sit down for a week!"

"She stood up all through the R.I. lesson," Cathy remembered. "I wonder if that was why!"

"Here's the cross-roads," Jane said some time later as she shortened Rebel's reins a little and prepared to turn right. "Daddy said that's the way to the town and that's the way to the market." She pointed with her whip. "This way to the stables."

There was quite a bustle at Wendover Stables when the girls arrived, and they slid down from their ponies and moved them over to a quiet corner until things settled down a bit. A tall lady in breeches and boots was heaving a rather plump little girl with pigtails up on to an equally plump pony, and trying to direct a small boy who was determined to mount from the wrong side, at one and the same time.

"Now, Wendy dear," she said. "Remember— left foot in the stirrup-iron, face towards your pony's tail. Left hand on the saddle pommel and swing yourself lightly up. Lightly, dear," she remonstrated. "Pickles doesn't like it when you arrive on his back like a sack of old potatoes— The other side, Colin! You *must* mount from the other side! No! Left foot in the stirrup, Colin—or you'll have to get on over his neck and finish up back to front, won't you?

"Now, Wendy, how did I tell you to hold the reins? It's no good screwing them up in a bunch like that, dear, or you'll never be able to guide

4

him. One in each hand—and just a minute while I get your fingers right. Pat, come and hold Pickles will you, dear, while I get Colin up in the saddle properly."

After a few minutes the excitement quietened down. A young efficient-looking girl came back with an outride and took the class of beginners into the indoor menage, while the more experienced riders led their mounts into the stables and started untacking them.

The tall lady put back a strand of hair from her face and breathed a sigh of relief.

Jane came over to her.

"I'm sorry to trouble you at such a busy time," she said. "But Saturday morning was the only time we could come in term-time."

The lady in breeches was only half-listening. She was running her eye over Rebel.

"I know that pony," she said suddenly. "It's Rebel, isn't it? I had her for a short time myself."

"Yes," Jane said. "We hoped that you'd remember her. We're trying to trace back all her previous owners. You know her name?"

"Rebel?" the riding school owner said. "Yes, it was on her bridle when I had her. Although we often called her Belle for short. Rebel tended to make her riders expect trouble, and horses can always sense if they know you're nervous. I didn't keep her long," the lady admitted. "She was too much of an unknown quantity for the kind of children I have here. Nice pony too. It was a pity."

"We bought her as Belle," Jane said. "We only found out her real name a short time ago."

"Scares easily, doesn't she?" the lady went on. "She had one of my children off. The child broke a collar bone. Parents were furious too. Other times she was as quiet as a lamb. Pity I didn't have the time to re-school her. Might have made something of her then."

"Did she only throw a child once?"

"Once is enough in my business," the lady pointed out. "After that none of the other children wanted to ride her."

"Where was she when it happened?" Jane asked.

"When she threw the child?" the lady said. "On an out-ride. We take them along Market Road past the almshouses and along Piggybank Lane. It's not built up out there. Plenty of lanes for the beginners, and leads into open country eventually where the older ones can have a good canter. My assistant was with them at the time. Had a good child on the pony too. Girl of fourteen who had been riding for years. I never did find out what really happened. It was Market Day and there were rather a lot of people about. Not that the mare had ever minded crowds, or noise either come to that. The children said there was some kind of excitement. Litter of pigs got out, I think, and they had a fine old time re-penning them. My girl waited with the riders at the side of the road for things to die down a bit. Didn't want to add to the general disturbance, you see.

Caused quite a traffic jam too. Suddenly the pony took off. Reared up and nearly had the child underneath her. Fortunately the girl had the sense to throw her weight forward—which helped a bit. Then the pony dropped down again, and up with her hind legs. Child wasn't expecting it. Came clean out of the saddle. Fell awkwardly and broke a collar bone. Could have happened to anyone."

"And afterwards?" Jane wanted to know.

"Policeman called an ambulance and got the child to hospital. Someone grabbed the grey's bridle, and my girl led her home. Quiet as a lamb by then, but the damage was done."

"And you got rid of her?" Jane finished.

"Yes," the lady said. "Nothing else to do really. Can't keep a pony with vice in this business. Never know where you are. It had happened a couple of times before, you see, but not with such drastic consequences. But I wasn't prepared to risk its happening again."

"Where did you get her from in the first place?" Jane asked.

"Bought her at a Horse Sale," the lady said. "I ought to have known better really. But she was a pretty mare and I was taken with her. Useful size too."

"What sale and when?" Jane wanted to know.

"Crampton," the lady said. "In the spring. Oh, must have been a couple of years ago."

"And you don't know who sold her?" Jane said.

"Must have it somewhere, I suppose," the lady

admitted. "But couldn't lay my hands on it after all this time. I expect the auctioneers could, if you could persuade them to turn it up. Sudden and Ryder it was. Of Crampton. You could see what they have to say."

They thanked her and turned to go.

"You want to watch her though, young lady," the riding mistress said in parting. "She looks quiet enough now but she can be a devil when she's roused."

"I wish we could find out what rouses her," Jane said. "That's the important thing, after all."

"I'm sorry I can't help you," the lady said. "I only had her a short time, as I told you, and I could never put my finger on it."

"Rather a wasted journey," Belinda said as they turned out of the stable yard.

"Not completely," Cathy argued. "We've got the next piece of the puzzle, if those auctioneers will tell us where Rebel came from."

The girls picnicked by a little stream on the way back, loosening the ponies' reins so that they could graze, and watering them in the shallows afterwards.

"We'll be back in good time to go shopping," Belinda said, glancing at her watch.

Jane snorted. The others didn't say anything out loud, but Belinda suddenly thought to herself:

"I'll just try it! I'll pray for Jane. I'll ask God to help her to stop being jealous of Mrs. Parminter and the baby and to be nice about it instead. And I'll see if it works."

Belinda would have been very surprised if she had known that Cathy was thinking and doing exactly the same thing!

"I think a green pram would be nice," Jane said suddenly, and the other two were so surprised that their jaws dropped and they stared at Jane with wide-open eyes.

"What on earth's the matter with you two?" Jane asked. "You look as if the Loch Ness Monster was about to climb out of the stream and eat you, or something."

"It's nothing," Belinda choked. "What were you saying about the pram?"

"I was saying," Jane said, "that I thought a green pram would be nice for the baby. Everyone seems to choose black or cream ones. It would be nice to be different."

"Yes, it would," Cathy stammered.

Belinda didn't say anything. She was thinking that it was probably wrong to feel so surprised when God answered your prayers in a really definite way.

Chapter 5

JANE IS CORNERED

"I'VE got the horses in for you, Miss."

Mr. Styles came forward to greet Sue Bright and Joy as they came into the stable yard.

"Thank you, Mr. Styles," Sue said. "I'll just check their girths and get Miss Wills mounted, and then we'll be off. Isn't it a lovely evening?"

"It is that," Mr. Styles agreed. "Given me a chance to do a bit of whitewashing today. It's as much as I can do to find the time to keep the place in order."

"I didn't know you kept pigs," Joy remarked, sniffing the clean smell of the newly limewashed sty to the left of the paddock gate.

"I don't now," Mr. Styles said. "Found they was too much trouble. I thought if I cleaned out the sty and knocked the partition down it would do for a tack room. I can do with a bit more space. I shall get round to finishing it some time. But the place is a bit much for me really. None of us get any younger, do we?"

"You're not thinking of selling up?" Joy said suddenly.

Sue looked at her friend in surprise.

"It's not as easy as that, Miss," Mr. Styles explained. "The property was left between me and my brother when my father died. Jim was proper put out about it too. He reckoned he should have had the larger share of father's estate, being the elder, you see, and perhaps he was right. There was bitter words at the funeral and I've never seen him since. But I can't sell out without his consent, you see, and he said he'll never agree to that. Not even if the place falls to pieces around my ears."

"Where does your brother live?" Sue asked.

"Outover somewhere," Mr. Styles said vaguely. "He don't have much to do with anyone these days, I hear. Bit touched in the head, some say, but I don't know about that."

"What made you ask Mr. Styles about selling the stables?" Sue asked her friend curiously as they guided their horses down the road which led towards open country. "Don't forget, Joy, heels down and shorten your reins a little, until you can feel the contact with his mouth."

"There's so much to remember at once," Joy complained. "And yet it looks so easy when *you* do it. . . . I haven't forgotten about your idea of setting up a Riding Centre with Uncle's money," she said in answer to Sue's question, when she had adjusted her position. "It did just occur to me that Mr. Styles's stable might be a pretty good place for it."

"For goodness' sake don't be influenced by me," Sue said hastily. "Just because I feel that a

Riding Centre would be a good idea, it doesn't necessarily mean it's the right thing for you to do."

"I know that," Joy said.

"If this motorway scheme is confirmed," Sue said, "Mr. Styles's brother won't have any choice about selling. The government will just put a compulsory purchase order on it."

"Do you think it will go through?" Joy asked. "There's a lot of local opposition to it."

"Bill is doing all he can to push the alternative scheme," Sue said, referring to her brother, who was a reporter on the local paper. "The editor of *The Echo* has given him a free hand. It skirts the village instead of cutting through one side. He thinks it's a much better idea."

"And it wouldn't touch Mr. Styles's property, would it?" Joy asked.

"No," Sue said. "Don't loll back in the saddle, Joy, straighten your back. And keep your hands low—your feet are much better. Let's trot a bit," she suggested. "Don't try and rise to the bump for the first few strides—do a sitting trot—you'll be firmer in the saddle that way."

"I'll take your word for it," Joy said, grinning wryly at her friend as she bumped unsteadily up and down.

"That was jolly good," Sue said approvingly a few minutes later, when the girls had slowed to a walk again. "You really looked as if you were in control, and you're getting the rhythm beautifully."

"Thank you for those few kind words, Ma'am," Joy said gratefully, settling herself more comfortably into the saddle.

"Going back to your money?" Sue said. "You have decided to use it in some way then? When we were talking about it last week you seemed half-inclined to give it all away."

"Yes," Joy said, "I was, but I came across some verses in Ecclesiastes the other day and now I'm not so sure. It went something like this: *Every man to whom God has given wealth and possessions, and power to enjoy them, should accept his lot and find enjoyment in his toil.* And it went on to say *This is the gift of God . . . and God will keep him occupied with joy in his heart.* I've been thinking that if God has given me this wealth, perhaps I ought to accept 'my lot' and find enjoyment in what He wants me to do with it. That didn't seem to be as if He meant me just to give the money away."

"It's always so hard to know exactly what God wants one to do," Sue remarked. Joy's horse was slouching along with his head down as she spoke. "Kick him on a bit, Joy, he's ambling along like an old man," she instructed.

"I made a mistake when I went to Africa," Joy said quietly, as she obediently applied her heels. "I don't want to make another one."

"But was it a mistake?" Sue questioned. "The way things turned out in the end? It's always difficult to tell."

"Talking about knowing what God wants one

to do," Joy said, "did you hear about the girls' experience at the Children's Home, when they offered to teach some of the kids to ride?"

"Yes," Sue laughed. "I gather Jane says it's the very last time she is ever going to try and do a good turn! A bit sweeping, I thought!"

"The trouble is we so often want to do spectacular things in connection with Christian service," Joy said thoughtfully, "when sometimes God's plan for us lies much nearer home."

"What do you mean, exactly?" Sue said.

"Well, take the sick man whom Jesus healed. He was dead keen to go with Jesus on his journeys afterwards, but Jesus said 'Go home to your friends and tell *them* how much the Lord has done for you.' It would have been much more exciting and satisfying to go around with Jesus than to just go home."

"But what's that got to do with the girls using their ponies for God?" Sue said.

"I don't really know," Joy said. "But it was just a thought."

"Do you feel like cantering?" Sue said. "There's a nice stretch of grass up here."

"Ooh-er!" Joy said. "What happens if I can't stop him?"

"That's what the reins are for," Sue reminded her patiently. "Anyway it's harder getting Mr. Styles's horses going than it is to stop them."

During the following week the question of the girls using their ponies came up again in a rather unexpected way.

A group of girls from Class 3 had been playing rounders during the dinner hour, but it
had proved somewhat exhausting and they
all threw themselves down on the grass for a
rest.

A rather plain girl called Mary Witter was
pulling tops off dandelion clocks and blowing
them idly into the air.

"Stop it, Mary," Jane complained. "It's all
getting up my nose. You'll make me sneeze."

Mary deliberately continued blowing until
Jane leaned forward and snatched the clock out
of her hand.

Mary stuck her tongue out at Jane, and at
once looked round for further dandelions.

"You are beastly, Mary," Jane said frankly.
"I don't wonder that no one likes you."

"Not many people like you either," Mary
retaliated. "You're too stuck up."

"I'm not stuck up," Jane denied hotly. "What
on earth do you mean?"

"What with your governess, and your horses,
and your father being a Major, and all that,"
Mary said. "Of course you're stuck up."

Jane's cheeks flamed. "I haven't got a governess now," she said coldly. "And I only had
lessons at home because I'd hurt my back. And
lots of people have horses, and I can't help it if
my father was in the army."

Cathy felt she had to come to Jane's rescue.
"I know we're lucky to have our own ponies,
Mary," she admitted. "But I can't see that makes

us 'stuck up'. Stuck up is when you think you're a jolly sight better than anyone else."

"Well, don't you think you are better than anyone else?" Mary's best friend, Penelope, broke in coolly.

"Of course not," Belinda said. "We don't think anything of the sort."

"But only stuck-up people ride ponies," Mary insisted, returning to the original taunt.

"Not everyone wants to ride," Belinda said. "Some people are afraid of horses."

"And some people just can't afford riding lessons," Sally Cox, a rather pleasant girl, put in quietly.

Cathy's heart gave a kind of leap, almost as if it was going to jump into her throat. Belinda and Jane went very quiet too. Cathy remembered her prayer. "Please God, show us if you want us to use the ponies in some way for You." Surely God didn't want them to ask that horrible Mary Witter and her friend Penelope if they'd like to ride the ponies sometimes? He couldn't really be suggesting that they should do that? There was a short silence.

"Well, people can save up," Jane said defensively, in reply to Sally's remark.

"It takes a long time to save up if you only get ten pence a week pocket money," Sally pointed out. "And then you really need the proper clothes, or at least a riding hat."

Cathy became very quiet. She could still remember the time when she had to save up

for an occasional ride with Mr. Styles, and how
she felt when she found Kelpie, apparently un-
used, in his lonely field.

Belinda moved over to sit beside Cathy.

"You don't think we ought . . . ?" she began
in an undertone. "I mean, you don't think God
means us to . . . ?" She didn't need to finish the
sentence.

"I don't know," Cathy admitted miserably.

"It must be lovely to have your own pony,"
Joan Cluff—a dark, rather lonely little girl with
pigtails—said wistfully. "I've got a kitten—but
it's not quite the same. I mean, a pony is a kind
of companion, isn't it? You wouldn't need to
have other people around if you'd got a pony
to talk to. It would be like having a special
friend."

"Yes, it is," Cathy agreed quickly. "I'm sure
they understand what you say to them and the
mood you're in too. Kelpie does anyway."

Belinda took a deep breath. "You can have
a go on Candy some time if you like, Joan,"
she said. "It won't be quite the same as having
a pony of your own, but it will be better than
nothing."

Cathy quickly followed Belinda's lead. "And
Sally can come and ride Kelpie," she said. "I'm
not absolutely marvellous at riding, but I can
teach you how to trot and canter, and the basic
aids and things like that."

Everyone then stared at Jane—especially
Mary and Penelope. Cathy and Belinda felt

rather sorry for her. They realized they had put her in a difficult position, but it was too late to back out. Jane always hated to be forced to do anything she didn't want to, and anyway Mary and Penelope were the two girls whom she most disliked.

"Perhaps we could start a kind of Saturday riding club," Cathy said helpfully. "For an hour or so in the morning or something like that. Then those people who really want to ride but find it's a bit expensive could come along and take turns on our ponies, while we gave you some tips on how to ride."

"Thanks for volunteering me," Jane hissed at Cathy, although Cathy somehow had the feeling that Jane was grateful for the way Cathy had helped her out of the situation.

Jane didn't sound very grateful after school though, when the three girls were alone.

"I'm absolutely fed up the way you've landed us with teaching that lumpy lot to ride," she exploded. "Just imagine poor old Rebel with ten-ton Mary splurged all over her back. Anyway she'll probably chuck her off," she said with considerable satisfaction.

"But I couldn't really help it," Cathy protested feebly.

"Anyway it was my fault in the beginning," Belinda admitted.

"You bagged Sally, and Cathy bagged Joan," Jane snorted. "And there was I left with the choice of offering to teach Mary or Penelope to ride. And what a choice. I could have banged your heads together. And how are we going to carry on the search for Rebel's owners if we're landed with a kind of Nursery School Riding Class every single Saturday morning?"

"Well, it needn't be every Saturday," Cathy pointed out. "And it will only be in the morning anyway."

"But why did you have to let us in for it?" Jane demanded. "That's what I can't understand."

"I thought it was God answering our prayer about using the ponies for someone else," Cathy said quietly. "If you really want to know."

"And I thought so too," Belinda admitted. "I wasn't very keen on the idea, but it seemed to me that we were meant to offer just the same."

"You two are nuts," Jane said simply. "How could we possibly be serving God by giving those two heavyweight puddings rides on our ponies? It would have been quite different with children from the Children's Home. They aren't properly well, so they ought to have some kind of a treat."

"I can't see we would have been serving God by giving the impression we were stuck up," Cathy said stubbornly. "And to refuse to let the girls share our ponies when some of them were so obviously longing to learn to ride. It might have been more exciting teaching disabled children, and made us feel more noble, if you know what I mean, but I have a feeling God might be more pleased with us for letting Mary Witter and Penelope Strange ride our ponies instead. And some of the others are awfully nice," she pointed out.

"Well, I'm glad you think God will be pleased," Jane snorted. "Because *I'm* certainly not!" and she heaved her satchel on to her shoulder and set off grumpily for Styles' Stable to collect Rebel.

"We've done it now," Belinda muttered gloomily to Cathy. "I can see we're in for a jolly evening."

"Perhaps she'll get over it on the way home," Cathy said hopefully as she waved the other two goodbye, but she knew that it was very unlikely.

Chapter 6

THE FIRST LESSON

"WE'RE going to have a pretty full day," Jane remarked to Belinda one Saturday morning a few weeks later as they were riding down to the village. "Thanks to you and Cathy getting us tied up in this riding lesson lark."

"But it's only in the morning," Belinda reminded her. "And it will probably be quite fun. Why have you got that long stick with binder cord tied on the end?" she asked curiously.

"That's my whip," Jane said coldly. "Instructors always have a whip when they stand in the middle of the menage."

"But we haven't got a menage," Belinda said sensibly. "And if you stand in the middle of the village green holding that, you're going to look a bit silly."

"We can mark out some boundaries with coats and things," Jane said. "And make a kind of circle so that the ponies follow round the outside."

Belinda could tell that Jane had put herself in charge of the riding sessions!

Cathy was waiting for them when they arrived at the open stretch of rather scrubby grass that bore the somewhat grand name of Bedborough

Village Green. There was also a group of about eight girls from the third form.

"Help!" Jane said, pulling a face. "It looks as if we're going to be kept busy! I never dreamed so many would turn up."

She swung herself down from her saddle and gave Rebel's reins to Belinda.

"Now," she said briskly. "How many of you have ever been on a horse before?"

Only Sally Cox put up her hand.

"I've ridden on a donkey at the seaside," Mary Witter said doubtfully.

Jane gave her a withering look. "I don't think that really counts, Mary," she said.

"But I expect you enjoyed it," Cathy put in quickly. "And that's the main thing. Donkeys and horses aren't all that different."

"Well, they've both got four legs and a tail," Jane conceded. "But I shouldn't have thought that a ride up and down the sands exactly qualified you for the British Show Jumping Championship."

"Don't be horrid, Jane," Belinda hissed, "or you'll put them off before we start!"

"First we want to form a roughly shaped ring —by marking the boundaries with our coats," Jane said. "Then we'll have Joan, Sally and Mary mounted, and I shall stand in the middle of the ring with my whip and tell you what to do. Mary can ride Rebel, and Joan Kelpie, and Sally Candy," she decided.

"I bet she hopes Rebel throws Mary off,"

Belinda muttered to Cathy as they paced out the ring.

It was quite a job getting Mary into the saddle. She had on very tight red jeans which threatened to split at the slightest provocation. Rebel was very fresh and just wouldn't stand still. She kept tossing her head up and down and switching her tail, and Mary didn't seem very keen on the idea of getting on top of her.

"Penelope can have first go if she likes," she offered generously, but Penelope wasn't anxious to take advantage of her friend's offer.

"Look, for goodness' sake stop arguing!" Jane said. "Or we shall never get anywhere."

"I'll give you a leg up," Belinda said to Mary. She cradled Mary's left foot in her hand and gave an enormous heave. Mary shot up in the air, went right over the top of Rebel's back and came down the other side in an undignified heap.

"What happened?" she asked in bewilderment, picking herself up from the ground.

"When you're given a leg up it's only to help you into the saddle," Jane said coldly. "Not to give you a chance to do circus acrobatics and mess about. Let her get up on that bank," she instructed Belinda. "Or we're going to spend the whole morning getting everyone mounted."

Cathy had helped Joan to mount Kelpie and shown her how to hold the reins, and Belinda had got Sally up on Candy without any difficulty. They both looked quite comfortable in the saddle;

it was only Mary who looked distinctly unhappy.

"I don't think I like it," she whined. "I want to get down."

"Of course you don't," Jane said briskly. "Here, you can let Sally go," she told Belinda, "and grab hold of Rebel's bridle for a bit. We don't want her galloping off across the common and she looks in a bit of a mood."

Mary paled and grasped the pommel with both hands, letting go of the reins.

"You mustn't loose the reins," Belinda warned her quietly. "They are your steering wheel and your brake. You wouldn't let go of a car's wheel if you were driving, would you?"

Mary reluctantly took one hand off the saddle and grasped the reins in a bunch.

"We'll just start by walking round the ring," Jane said bossily, taking up her position in the middle. "That will give you a chance to get your seats and to begin to feel comfortable on the ponies."

"I don't think I shall ever feel comfortable," Mary whimpered, leaning back in the saddle as if it were an armchair.

"You must sit up, Mary," Jane said. "Keep your back straight and don't loll."

"It's so wobbly," Mary complained. "I didn't think it would be so wobbly."

Sally was managing very nicely, and Joan's eyes were shining as she gave herself to Kelpie's easy movements.

"Well done, Sally, well done, Joan," Jane said

approvingly. "Shorten up your reins a little and keep your elbows in."

"We're not going to jump gates and things, are we?" Mary asked nervously. "Because I don't think I'd like that at all."

"Nor would Rebel," Jane said shortly. "No, Mary, I don't really think you're quite up to jumping yet."

"You're doing quite well," Belinda said comfortingly to Mary. "Don't worry. Jane always sounds bossy but she doesn't mean it, really."

Mary nodded, grateful for the small comfort. Now that she had completed two circles without falling off, her heart was beating a little more steadily, but she licked her dry lips nervously.

"Now we'll practise using the reins," Jane said, flicking her whip quite unnecessarily, just because she liked the sound of it. "If you want to turn right you use the right rein, and at the same time use your left leg and the inside of your right heel to push your pony over. If you want to turn left you use your right leg and your left rein. It's really quite easy. We'll practise with each of you in turn making a circle round me. First we'll make a right-hand circle. You start, Sally."

Cathy and Belinda stood and watched while Sally turned Candy in a circle. She made quite a good job of it. Joan was a little less confident, but Cathy put a guiding hand on the rein and showed her what to do.

Rebel was getting bored, and pawed the ground crossly before she would even walk on, and then tried to break into a trot, which nearly unseated Mary, but Belinda stayed close beside her and gradually Mary relaxed and became a little more confident. Then they did some suppling-up exercises.

After about a quarter of an hour Cathy suggested that a second group should have a ride.

"Here! You can have a go at this, Belinda," Jane said, throwing down her whip. "I must have run miles round and round this circle. I feel quite puffed out."

"All right," Belinda agreed, "But you'd better come and lead Rebel. Just walking around in circles isn't exactly in her line."

Jane came over and took Rebel's bridle and gave Alison, her new rider, a few instructions about sitting well down into the saddle, and feeling the pony's mouth with the reins. Suddenly, without any warning, Rebel bunched herself into a taut mass of muscle, laid her ears back and started to back away vigorously from Jane's restraining hand.

"She's off again!" Jane shouted. "Come and help me hold her, Belinda!"

Belinda responded quickly, and came running across the grass to Jane's assistance.

"Just sit tight, Alison," she called. "You'll be quite safe with Jane and me holding her."

Alison wasn't sure that she believed them and she didn't like the feel of the plunging pony beneath her, but she had the good sense to realize that it wasn't exactly the right moment to suggest that she would prefer to get down.

Belinda and Jane were fighting Rebel with all their strength, secretly afraid that she might break away from them, and gallop off with her very inexperienced rider. Cathy wondered if she should go and help as well but decided she had better keep a restraining hand on Candy and Kelpie in case they should follow Rebel's bad example.

Rebel was showing the whites of her eyes and her breath was coming in great shuddering gasps. She tried desperately to snatch her head from the girls' grasp and danced upon her toes, the nervous sweat already beginning to darken her neck.

"Whatever is the matter?" Alison asked anxiously. "It wasn't anything I did, was it?"

"No, you didn't do anything," Belinda assured her breathlessly. "She gets like this sometimes; for no reason at all as far as we can see.

"Let's lead her over the other side of the green," she suggested to Jane. "If we get her moving it will give her something to think about, and it will be easier to keep her under control."

Jane nodded and they strained all their weight backwards against the fretting Rebel, in order to make her walk slowly. The pony was only too glad to be on the move.

As the girls crossed the green the pony gradually calmed down, and by the time they had reached the bus shelter on the far side, she was almost herself again.

Jane patted her mare's damp neck. Rebel nuzzled Jane gently with her nose.

"What *is* the matter, girl?" Jane asked her helplessly. "I only wish you could tell us what frightens you so."

Now the crisis was over Alison began to view herself in the guise of a heroine who had successfully controlled a wild and plunging pony with courage and calmness!

"I thought she was going to run away with me," she told the others excitedly. "But I managed to stay in the saddle, and we stopped her between us."

Jane and Belinda exchanged grins but were thankful Alison hadn't panicked, which would only have made matters worse. Mary Witter, who had kept a safe distance away, now came up.

"I expect it was that lorry that frightened her," she said importantly.

"Rebel isn't traffic-shy," Jane said shortly. "So it certainly wasn't that. It was more likely to have been your scarf. It's a simply ghastly colour and you keep flapping it around."

"Trees," Cathy said thoughtfully. "I suppose it couldn't have been the wind in the trees? There's that huge oak in the middle of the green and the wind is making an awful lot of noise blowing through the leaves."

Everyone looked over to the huge oak tree that stood right in the centre of the village green.

The trunk was about sixteen feet in circumference and you couldn't even see round the other side. It had been there for centuries and there was some rumour that a royal fugitive had once hidden in it and thereby escaped his enemies, though no one knew if the story was true.

"I suppose an acorn didn't fall on her?" Sally said. "There's lots of them on the ground. I saw some pigs eating them the other day."

"Acorns don't fall off this time of year, do they?" someone asked; but no one was good enough at botany to be able to give a definite answer.

"Look!" Jane said. "Rebel isn't *that* nervous! It's nothing as simple as that. Anyway, I think we'll move the ring over this side of the green— just in case we have another performance. My arms are just about pulled out of their sockets. I don't feel like facing any more of her mystery frights just yet."

Everyone helped to move the ring, Belinda once more took up her position in the centre and the lesson proceeded. Rebel behaved perfectly although Jane, Belinda and Cathy all kept a wary eye on her.

"I think it's time we let the last two girls have a go," Belinda said, after she had repeated Jane's lesson with the second set of girls. "You can take over, Cathy. It's good practice if we all have a go."

No one seemed over-keen to ride Rebel, so Jane stood holding her while Kelpie and Candy obediently carried their new riders around the improvised menage.

"We'll have to go now," Jane said at last. "We ought to get back and give the ponies a feed and a bit of a rest if we're going to take them to Crampton this afternoon."

"Can we help?" Sally and Joan begged.

"Well, not now," Jane said. "But you can some other day. When we're not so pushed for time. And we'll teach you to tack-up and to groom the ponies as well."

"It's jolly nice of you," Mary said gruffly. "I didn't really think you would let us, when we were talking the other day. I thought you'd back out or make some kind of excuse."

"We wouldn't break a promise," Cathy said indignantly.

"It's been lovely," Sally told them. "I'm going to get a book out of the library and swot up all you've taught us. I think you're ever such a good teacher, Jane."

Jane blushed with pleasure.

"Well, thanks," she said awkwardly. "And I think you've all done very well for a first lesson. Even you, Mary," she conceded generously.

"Can we have another lesson soon?" Penelope wanted to know.

"Yes," Jane said. "But I'm not quite sure when. We'll fix it at school."

Everyone chorused their thanks.

"Doesn't it make you feel nice inside when you've done something good," Jane remarked a little smugly as the three friends trotted back through the village.

"I've noticed that too," Cathy said. "Especially if it's something that you didn't much want to do in the beginning."

Everyone was quiet, then Jane said suddenly: "Mother is ill."

"How ill?" Cathy asked quickly.

"Not hospital ill," Jane said. "But in bed."

"I thought she was only resting," Belinda said. "Because of the baby."

"It is because of the baby," Jane agreed. "But it's not just that she's got to rest. She's got something called toxaemia. It can make both mother and the baby quite ill. That's why she's got to rest."

"What's toxaemia?" Belinda wanted to know.

"It's a kind of poisoning," Jane explained. "Something to do with the blood I think. Daddy was telling me about it last night."

"I expect she'll be all right if she rests," Cathy said comfortingly.

"Do you think it's because of me?" Jane asked. She sounded worried.

"Because of you?" Belinda was puzzled. "What on earth do you mean? How could it be?"

"Because I was horrid to mother," Jane said. "Because I didn't really want the baby to be born."

"That's just silly," Cathy said. "It hasn't got anything to do with it."

"How do you know?" Jane demanded.

"It couldn't possibly have anything to do with it," Cathy insisted.

"It might be God," Jane said. "He knew I didn't want the baby. Perhaps He's punishing me."

"He wouldn't be particularly punishing *you* anyway," Belinda pointed out. "It would be your father and mother who would be punished."

"It would be me as well," Jane said in a choking voice. "You see I do want the baby really— now I do. I couldn't bear it if anything happened to Mother and the baby—just because I was so beastly about it in the beginning."

"God isn't like that," Cathy said positively. "He doesn't punish people like that. He loves us, Jane! Don't you understand! He doesn't ever want bad things to happen to us. It makes Him ten times more unhappy than it makes us."

"Anyway I expect Mrs. Parminter and the baby will be perfectly all right," Belinda said comfortingly. "Lots of mothers have to rest before their babies come. There's nothing serious about that. I think you're just worrying about nothing. You just see, Jane. Everything will be all right."

"I do hope so," Jane said. "Or I shall feel it's all my fault."

"But I do think that you ought to be especially nice to Mrs. Parminter from now on," Cathy said. "Perhaps it's a good thing that you're a bit worried—it will make you more careful about upsetting her. And every time you feel you're getting jealous you must quickly ask the Lord Jesus to take the feeling away, and say or do something nice instead so that you get the jealous feeling right out of your mind."

"I'll try," Jane promised. "It always seems easy when I haven't got anything to be jealous about, and I feel the way I'm feeling now, but it comes on so suddenly—before I have time to think."

"That's the trouble with most sins," Cathy agreed. "Bad temper, and being cheeky, and telling lies, and all the rest of it. They happen so quickly you don't often have time to stop them, and the awful thing is that you don't really want to stop them at the time."

"I'm really glad we let the girls from school have a ride," Belinda said, changing the subject. "And I'm sure it was the right thing to do. Even if we weren't very pleased about it at first."

"I wonder if that auctioneer at Crampton will let us know the name of Rebel's previous owner," Jane said thoughtfully. "If he doesn't, we're going to be in a spot."

"I'm glad I'm coming to lunch," Cathy remarked. "We can set off to Crampton immediately afterwards."

Chapter 7

THE BLACKSMITH'S CLUE

THE clerk at the office of Sudden and Ryder —the auctioneers at Crampton—looked back through the records until he discovered the entry referring to the purchase of Rebel by the Wendover Riding School. "Here it is," he said triumphantly. "The mare was sold by a Mr. R. H. Collins from Shipping Camden. The address is just given as The Grange. 'Grey mare 14.2'—that would be it, wouldn't it?"

"Yes, it would," Jane said. "Thank you very much. You've been ever so helpful."

"You do realize that there is no come-back on the previous owner for anything that may be wrong with the mare?" the clerk said. "Once the hammer has fallen at the auction the pony becomes the legal property of the buyer. It's up to him to make sure that she is sound in every way before he bids for her."

"Oh, it's nothing like that," Jane assured him. "Rebel is perfectly sound. It's just that she seems to be frightened sometimes, and we thought if we could trace right back through her previous owners we might be able to discover the reason."

"I see," the clerk said. "Well I hope you're successful in your search."

"I don't think we'd better go over to Shipping Camden now," Jane said to the other two girls when she came out of the office and told them the news. "For one thing I'm not quite sure where it is, and it's getting rather late, and for another I'm not too happy about Rebel's back shoe. It's a bit loose and I think I ought to go and have it fixed. I don't want her going lame."

"I wonder if the blacksmith will still be working when we get back?" Cathy said. "I suppose he must take some time off, and it is Saturday."

"If not I shall have to leave it until after school on Monday," Jane said. "We could walk down to Bible Class tomorrow afternoon, I suppose. It wouldn't hurt us for once."

"Miss Bright and Joy are a bit disappointed about the attendance at Bible Class lately," Cathy said. "Especially with our age group. We've only had about half a dozen for the last three weeks. I can't think what has happened to them all."

"Hardly any of the girls at school go," Belinda said. "I suppose we ought to ask them."

"It's so difficult," Cathy complained. "I never know what to say. And they always think it must be dull, and never believe you when you say that it isn't."

"I used to think it would be dull," Jane said. "Do you remember? I know I said I'd give it a try and if it was dull I jolly well wouldn't go any more."

"But you still come," Cathy said.

"Yes," Jane admitted. "I like it. And it's surprising what you learn. I sometimes think that God sits down and works bits out specially for me. Like that bit about Saul. It was jolly funny."

"It just happened that we're reading it at the moment in our Bible Notes," Cathy pointed out. "And I expect it fitted a lot of other people as well for lots of different reasons. The Bible is like that."

"How do you mean?" Jane said.

"Well . . ." Cathy was trying to think of a way of explaining. "You know you told me that you were feeling awfully jealous about the baby and so it made you feel bad when you realized how absolutely foul being jealous could make you? Because you read about Saul being jealous of David."

"Yes," Jane said.

"Well . . . " Cathy was screwing up her face in an effort to put what she wanted to explain, into words. "Perhaps someone else who was reading it had been tactless—talking loudly about the good marks that a girl had got in the Maths exam in front of a girl who was absolutely hopeless—so that the hopeless girl couldn't help but feel jealous. Surely if she was reading the same bit of the Bible that you read, she would realize that she ought to have been more thoughtful—and considered the feelings of the other person a bit more."

"You're thinking about the women who sung that song when Saul was listening?" Belinda said

6

helpfully. "About Saul having killed thousands of his enemies but David killing tens of thousands?"

"Yes," Cathy said. "I always thought it was pretty silly of them, they might have known it would make Saul mad. You see God can speak to lots of different people in lots of different ways—through reading the same part of the Bible. Providing you're prepared to listen to Him, that is," she finished.

"Rebel's shoe *is* loose," Belinda remarked. "I can hear it clinking every time she puts her foot down."

Fortunately the blacksmith was still in his forge and the girls didn't have to wait long for him to have a look at Rebel's feet.

"She needs a complete refit really, Miss," he said. "But I'll just fix this one for the time being and perhaps you can bring her in again at the beginning of the week."

"Thanks a lot," Jane said gratefully.

Rebel stood quietly while the blacksmith removed the loose shoe and trimmed her hoof.

"Nice little mare," the man went on conversationally. "Haven't had her long, have you?"

"About six months," Jane said. "Kelpie was getting a bit small for me."

The blacksmith nodded, his back bent low over the mare's foot which he held between his knees.

"Had a nasty cut on her pastern some time ago, I see. Lucky it didn't lame her. You can still see the scar."

Jane bent down to have a look.

"Do you know I've never noticed that before!" she said in amazement. "I suppose it's because she's grey. The mark doesn't show very clearly."

"Can't hide anything from me," the blacksmith boasted. "All my life I've had to do with horses' feet. It's not much that misses my eye."

"I wonder if it was on the vet's report," Jane said. "Daddy asked him to go over the pony before we bought her."

"I expect it was," the blacksmith said. "But as it had completely healed there was nothing to bother about."

"But how did she get it?" Cathy said slowly. "That's what I would like to know."

"Perhaps it was wire," Belinda said. "She could have got herself tied up."

The blacksmith inspected the scar again. "Too clean for wire," he argued. "But it was a nasty cut all the same."

"The plot thickens," Jane said as they made their way back to the farm for a late tea. "Do you think there is any connection between the scar and Rebel's fear?"

"I shouldn't be surprised," Belinda said. "At least it's a clue. Fancy us not noticing it before."

"A clue to what?" Cathy said. "That's what we've got to find out."

"Do you want to stay to tea?" Jane asked Cathy when the girls reached the farm. "Mother is in bed so we'll have to get it ourselves."

"If you're sure I shan't be in the way," Cathy said.

"You and Belinda untack the horses and turn them out," Jane said, "and I'll go and see what's what."

There was no one in the farm kitchen as Jane came through the big studded door, so she went quietly up the stairs to the front bedroom that Major Parminter and his new wife now shared. Mrs. Parminter was lying propped up with pillows and Major Parminter sat on the side of the bed holding his wife's hand. Neither of them noticed Jane standing in the doorway.

"I seem such a fraud lying here," Mrs. Parminter was saying, "when I feel perfectly well. And I hate the idea of you and the girls having to get your own meals."

"Don't be silly, darling," the Major said. "All I want is for you to be fit and strong so that you can cope with our youngster when he decides to make his entry into the world."

"You are pleased about the baby, aren't you?" Mrs. Parminter said, pressing his hand.

"I'm delighted," Jane's father said. "I can't remember being so excited since the day when Jane was born."

"I hope it's a son," Mrs. Parminter said. "I do hope it's a son."

"So do I," Major Parminter said.

As Jane stood listening, she became aware of the Lord Jesus speaking to her angry troubled heart, but she didn't want to listen. The sight of her beloved father sitting and holding his wife's hand gave her a left-out feeling that made her throat thicken and her eyes fill with tears. She felt very miserable.

"I hope it's a son," her stepmother had said.

"So do I," her father had agreed. Her father wanted a son! He didn't want her—Jane—any more. Everyone would love this new baby and no one cared about her. She was just a nuisance and an outsider and she couldn't bear it. She turned away.

It was a pity Jane didn't wait to hear the rest of her father's sentence.

"I hope it's a son, too," he said. "For Jane's sake. I can't help hoping that she will be my only girl. We've always meant so much to each other. It will be much easier for her to accept a new brother."

Jane tiptoed along the landing and silently opened her bedroom door. She flung herself down on her bed in a tumult of tears.

"I can't help being jealous," she sobbed. "And no one really understands! I wish Daddy had never married Miss Beckford and I wish the baby wasn't coming and I wish I'd never got better and been able to walk again! Then they would have had to love me and no one else would have taken my place!"

The door opened and Belinda came in. She stopped in surprise when she saw Jane lying across the bed and heard her sobs.

"Whatever is the matter?" she asked in concern.

"Go away," Jane said. "I don't want any tea. You and Cathy can help yourselves."

"Don't be silly," Belinda said. "Of course you want some tea. And your father and mother will think it funny if you don't come down."

"I don't care what they think," Jane muttered. "And she's not my mother anyway."

"Oh dear," Belinda sighed. "It's that again."

"Yes it is," Jane said. "And I know you think I'm awful and I just don't care. You don't know what it's like."

Belinda sat down on the bed.

"I know you've got a father and mother who love you very much," she said slowly. "And they're here right now. But you just don't want their love and you turn your back on them. I wish my mother and father were here. I don't think you realize sometimes how much I miss them."

Jane stopped crying and lifted her tear-stained face from the pillow in surprise.

Belinda had walked over to the window and was staring out. She was biting her lip and she had her back to Jane.

Jane scrambled off the bed and went and put her arm round her friend.

"I'm sorry, 'Linda," she said. "I never thought. I am a selfish beast."

"You're not really," Belinda said. "I couldn't expect you to understand."

"But I do," Jane insisted. "I'd just die if I had to be parted from Daddy."

"You wouldn't die," Belinda said. "You'd just have to put up with it. And most of the time you'd find you'd get used to it in a funny kind of way."

"But you'll be going out to stay with them in the summer holidays," Jane reminded her friend. "And it's not all that long now."

"I know," Belinda said. "I'm just being silly."

Jane wiped her eyes on her sleeve and gave a vigorous sniff.

"Cathy will be wondering what has happened to us," she said. "We are a pair of miseries."

Belinda hesitated. "Would you think it very daft if we just said a prayer before we go down?" she said. "I think it would help."

Jane nodded. "All right," she said.

The girls knelt down by Jane's bed.

"Look, God," Jane said, after a moment's quiet. "I really am sorry about being jealous again. I didn't think it was going to come on like that—so suddenly. I'm sorry I wouldn't let you help me too. Please forgive me—and please comfort Belinda and help us to be specially nice to her so that she doesn't miss her parents too much. And forgive me for being a selfish pig and not noticing."

There was a short pause and then Belinda said:

"Please God, help Jane not to be jealous, and to be pleased about the baby when it comes. And forgive me for being such a misery and keep Mummy and Daddy safe until I can be with them again."

When the girls arrived downstairs they found Cathy standing alone in the kitchen, looking rather forlorn.

"Where on earth have you two been?"

"We've been praying," Jane said.

"But what a funny time to choose," Cathy said. "You might have told me. I thought we were going to have tea."

"We are," Jane said. "I'll just go and see if Mother and Dad have had theirs."

"She needn't make so much noise about it," Cathy remarked as Jane thundered up the stairs. "They'll think we're bringing the ponies up too. She is funny, isn't she?" she said to Belinda. "You never know what she'll do next."

At Bible Class the following afternoon Joy was talking to the girls about Guidance. She had decided to tell them about the money that had been left to her and how she was wondering in what way God wanted her to use it.

Everyone was very interested.

"I'd buy a new saddle," Jane said promptly. "And one of those super sheepskin covers to go under it."

Joy laughed. "You could buy a great number of saddles with the money that Uncle has left me," she said. "That's why I am so concerned to use it in the right way."

"I hope that God hurries up and tells you," Belinda said. "I should be dying to know, if I were you."

"I *am* dying to know," Joy agreed. "Perhaps that is why He spoke to me last night in the way He did."

"Really speaking?" Cathy asked, wide-eyed.

"As good as speaking," Joy said. "I was feeling rather unsettled about the whole matter and wishing I could be quite sure what I was meant to do and I turned to the book of Habakkuk and started reading it."

"I've never heard of it," Belinda said. "Is it in the Bible?"

"Yes," Joy said. "It's right at the end of the Old Testament and it's not a book we seem to read very often. But this is what it said. *If the vision seems slow, wait for it; it will surely come, it will not delay.*"

"Gosh!" Jane said. "It was like real speaking, wasn't it?"

"Yes," Joy said. "It was. That is why I thought I would share it with you. And then when the 'vision' does come I'll be able to tell you what it is."

"It makes life pretty exciting, doesn't it?" Jane said. "I mean, knowing that God is really in touch, and at the right moment He'll tell us what to do."

"I'm glad you feel that way, Jane," Joy said. "I do too."

"If He is in touch all the time," Belinda said, "does He know about the little things too? Things like not having many people at Bible Class and what we should do about it."

"Of course He knows," Joy said. "But He still wants us to talk to Him about it, so that if there is anything we are meant to do about it, He can tell us what it is."

"I don't see there is anything we *can* do," Jane said. "You can't make people come to Bible Class if they don't want to, can you?"

"No," Joy said. "But God can sometimes make them want to come. That's a bit different."

"I suppose it's like catching a horse," Cathy said thoughtfully. "If you take a bit of apple or carrot to the field with you, he will want to come to you, then you can slip the halter on without any fuss. You can't force his head into it against his will."

"We'd better take some carrot and apples to school," Jane said. "And see if it works with the girls in our form, about coming to Bible Class."

"Perhaps you're doing that already," Joy suggested quietly; but even when the girls pressed her, she wouldn't explain what she meant.

Chapter 8

THE LAST PIECE OF THE JIGSAW

"I wonder why it's so much harder to like some people than others?" Jane asked Belinda as they were riding to school one morning near the end of term.

"You mean people like Mary and Penelope?" Belinda said.

"Yes," Jane agreed.

"Perhaps some people find it hard to like us?" Belinda suggested.

Jane looked astounded. "I don't see how they can," she argued. "I mean . . . well . . . we're quite nice really . . . and ordinary . . . if you know what I mean."

"We're not always nice," Belinda pointed out. "In fact I was absolutely horrible to Penelope last week when she jabbed Candy's mouth just because she lost her footing."

"I should think so too," Jane said indignantly. "It's nearly time the silly goon had learned that you can't balance yourself on a horse by hanging on for dear life to the reins!"

"But she didn't do it on purpose." Belinda defended the absent Penelope. "It would have been different if she had done."

"Do you think there really are people who don't

like us?" Jane said. "That's absolutely awful. You like me, don't you?" she demanded.

"Of course I like you," Belinda said reassuringly. "And so does Cathy, and Sally and Joan—oh, and lots of other people."

"And I like you," Jane said, with surprising candour.

"But I don't think God gives us much credit for liking people who like us," Belinda said slowly. "I think it's liking people who don't like us that makes Him pleased."

"But that's a lot harder," Jane argued.

"I know it is," Belinda said. "And I'm not much better at it than you are."

"I don't see why we have to *like* Mary and Penelope," Jane said. "I think it's jolly decent of us to let them ride our ponies anyway. I don't see why we should like them as well."

"Well, I think we ought to try," Belinda said. "And see if we can stop being horrid to them. After all, they can't help being fat, and spotty, and not very nice. And they must know that most people at school don't like them, and don't choose them for their team and things like that. They'd be ever so pleased if we treated them like real friends."

"You have the horridest ideas," Jane complained.

"It wasn't my idea," Belinda denied. "It was in St. Luke I think—it stuck in my mind. It said something about 'If you love only those that love you—don't expect any reward. Anyone can do

that. You must love those people you don't like'—
or something like that. I thought of Mary and
Penelope straight away," she admitted.

"They all seem to like coming to the riding
classes," Jane said. "It's a pity we haven't got
a few more ponies so that they could ride for
longer. Some of them are getting quite good,
considering they've only had about five lessons."

"What will you do about the lessons during the
holidays?" Belinda asked. "When I go out to stay
with Mummy and Daddy."

"I haven't really thought," Jane said. "Would
we be able to use Candy if we decided to go on
with it?"

"Yes, I think so," Belinda said after a short
pause. "But you will take care of her, won't you?"
She patted the pony's sleek neck affectionately,
and Candy twitched her ears in acknowledgement.

"Of course we will," Jane said. "She'll need
some exercise anyway, to keep her fit."

"It's funny without Mrs. Parminter around."
Belinda changed the subject. "Are you going to
see her in hospital?"

"Not until the baby is born," Jane said.
"Daddy said it's better not to. I hope she'll be all
right," she said worriedly.

"I didn't think people went into hospital until
the baby was due to come," Belinda said. "Why
couldn't she stay at home and rest? Like she did
at first."

"They want to keep an eye on her," Jane said.
"In case anything goes wrong."

"I'm sure it won't," Belinda said. "So try not to worry too much."

"I do try," Jane said. "But I can't help worrying. It would be dreadful if the baby died or something horrible like that."

"I'm sure the baby won't die," Belinda said. "It's nearly time for it to come, isn't it? Just think what fun it's going to be when you have it at home. You'll be able to teach it to ride."

Jane giggled. "Well, not quite yet," she said. "I don't think you can start until it's about three."

"We must fix up with Cathy about Saturday afternoon," Belinda said, glad that she had made Jane laugh. "It looks as if we shall be free at last, and I'm longing to go to Shipping Camden, aren't you? Perhaps at last we'll find out what frightens Rebel, and why."

"And then we've got to re-school her," Jane pointed out. "That's easier said than done."

Saturday dawned bright and clear and, after a busy riding lesson in the morning, Jane, Belinda and Cathy had a quick lunch and set out on what they hoped would be the last lap of their search.

"Daddy has drawn me a map," Jane said. "I only hope I can follow it. He says that The Grange looks as if it's rather off the beaten track."

Major Parminter's description of The Grange proved to be an accurate one. It took the girls nearly an hour to find the rambling old house hidden amongst the trees about a mile outside the village of Shipping Camden.

"It looks deserted," Cathy said. "The trees are all overgrown, and the grass in this track is a mile high. No one can possibly live here."

"Well, the auctioneer gave me the right address," Jane insisted. "I saw it in his book. And this is The Grange," she said, pointing to the rusted sign that was half-hanging from the gate-post.

"It gives me the creeps," Belinda said with a shiver. "I'm glad we've got the horses with us."

"Let's get off," Jane suggested. "And go and investigate."

"No fear," Belinda said. "I'm going to stay mounted—ready for a quick getaway."

The drive was overgrown with grass and moss, and the trees hung over it, making a dark tunnel. The ponies moved their ears backwards and forwards questioningly as they picked their way almost silently towards the house.

"It's completely empty," Jane said in surprise as they reined-in by the front steps. "Let's go round to the back."

There was a stable block at the rear of the house, and a dilapidated dove-cote leaned drunkenly at a dangerous angle. But there was no sign of human life. Only the bees hovered busily over a cascade of late roses that covered one side of the stable block, and birds flew importantly hither and thither picking busily at insects hidden in the cracks between the cobbles.

"So that is that!" Jane said with a disappointed sigh.

"Was you looking for someone?" The voice seemed over-loud in the silence of the stable yard. Jane swung round in her saddle to see an elderly bent little man, with a shock of untidy white hair, staring at them curiously. For a moment he vaguely reminded her of someone, and she wondered if she had seen him before somewhere.

"Well, yes we were actually," Jane said, her heart beating a little faster with the surprise of the stranger's sudden appearance. "But there doesn't seem to be anyone here," she pointed out.

"They's been gone a twelvemonth or more," the man said. "And I don't know where they's gone to neither."

"It was a Mr. Collins, wasn't it?" Jane asked. "And he used to break-in horses."

"That's right," the man agreed. "I used to help 'un sometimes."

"Did you really?" Jane said, wondering if there might be a ray of hope in the situation after all. "And do you remember any of the horses that you helped break? Enough to recognize them, I mean."

The man nodded. "I'd know some of them," he declared. "Especially the bad 'uns. They be the ones you remember most."

He studied Rebel carefully as he was speaking, and then came forward slowly, laid his hand on Rebel's rump and ran it slowly down her left hind leg. His fingers searched gently for the scar on the pastern, hardly visible amongst the hair. He straightened his back. "I remember that one," he declared with a nod. "Proper little devil her were. Especially after her accident."

Jane felt breathless with excitement and the others were staring wide-eyed at the little man, hanging on his every word.

"Her accident?" Jane asked. "What accident?"

"Wiv that old sow," the man said slowly. "Her were a proper menace, were that old sow," he remembered. "Specially when her had a litter."

"Pigs!" Cathy breathed. "So that's what frightens her! I can't think why we never suspected."

"But there weren't always pigs around," Jane denied. "At least I don't think so . . ." she amended, feeling a little unsure of herself.

"Look 'ere," the old man said. "I can't stand here talking all day—with my roomatism. If you like to come and have a dish of tay with me in my cottage, you're welcome. Then I can tell you about the mare. It's quite a long story."

The girls looked at each other and nodded. They had been in the saddle for some time, and could do with stretching their legs.

It seemed funny drinking tea out of chipped white cups in the old man's little cottage which was tucked away at the rear of the house.

"Isn't it sweet?" Cathy said admiringly. "Does it belong to you?"

The old man shook his head. "Goes with the

house," he said. "When her's sold I shall have to go."

"Surely they couldn't turn you out?" Jane said indignantly. "I should complain to someone about it if I were you."

"But about the pony—" Belinda said. "I'm dying to know what happened."

The old man sat down and started to stir his tea.

"Her were just about half-broken," he said. "And a proper little devil 'er were. Full of sperit like—but no vice, you understand. Her were turned out in the long field, along with some others but her was always right curious—couldn't bear to miss anything that were going on.

"Master turned the old sow and her piglets out in the meadow next door and the mare jumped the hedge—just for devilment, you know, and apparently 'er must 'ave chased after one of the old sow's piglets, leastways that's all we could think of. The old sow went for her. Praper vicious they can be when they're roused. Caught the mare's foot just on the pastern. Tore it apart, 'er did, and the mare squealing like a mad thing.

"Master and I were on the scene pretty sharp-ish, and we got the mare away. Her foot were a nasty mess. Couldn't work her for a couple of months. The vet did a good job though. Don't hardly show do it?—only for those who know where to look."

"And what happened then?"

"When 'er was fit we started breaking 'er

again," the old man said. "But 'er was mortal feared of pigs from that day onwards. Quiet as a lamb 'er'd be until 'er saw or smelt that old sow around, then 'er would go like a mad thing."

"Don't I know it?" Jane said. "But it's *any* pig, you know, not just the sow that bit her."

"Horses have long memories," the old man said. "There's not much they ferget, I reckon."

"Poor Rebel," Cathy said. "She must have been absolutely terrified. And fancy her never forgetting it—even now."

"It's going to take a lot of time and patience to wipe it out of her mind," Jane said.

"But why has she never played up on the farm?" Belinda questioned.

"Because we haven't got any pigs, have we, silly?" Jane reminded her. "Everything else I should think, but just not pigs. Daddy isn't keen on them."

"Has Mr. Styles got pigs?" Cathy said. "She has played up there a couple of times."

"He used to keep them," Jane said. "Until recently."

"Who's that you said?" the old man asked slowly.

"Mr. Styles," Jane said. "He keeps a riding stable in Bedborough, and we leave our ponies there during the day when we've ridden them to school. Why? Do you know him?"

"I ought to," the old man said, scratching his head. "He's me own brother."

"Is he really?" Jane said. "Well, isn't that a

coincidence! Then your name must be Mr. Styles too?"

"Jim Styles," their new friend told them. "Me brother is Bill."

Jane, Cathy and Belinda looked at each other and felt a little uncomfortable. They didn't quite know what to say. They had remembered about the family quarrel, and the fact that Bill Styles and his brother weren't friends.

"How is Bill doing?" Jim Styles asked.

"He's all right," Jane said carefully. "But he finds the stables a bit much for him now he's getting older, I think."

Jim nodded. He picked up his cup and took a gulp of tea. There was an awkward pause.

"Look here," Jane said. "I know it's none of my business but it does seem stupid, holding on to a quarrel that happened years ago. Wouldn't it be more sensible to make it up?"

Cathy and Belinda pulled faces at each other behind Jim Styles's back. They thought Jane had rather a cheek interfering in the Styles family quarrel, when she'd only known Jim Styles for about half an hour.

"What do you know about the quarrel?" Jim growled at Jane. "And what cause have you to start meddling in my affairs?"

"I don't know much about the quarrel," Jane admitted. "Only that it was something to do with the house and you won't let your brother sell it. And that's a pity because, you see, Joy would probably buy it otherwise, and we could start a

Christian Riding Centre, but as it is, there's nowhere else suitable and so the vision seems slow and she's got to wait for it, but God said it's going to come in the end, but I only wish it would hurry up."

Jim Styles stared at Jane in bewilderment, trying hard to understand what she was talking about.

"You're making it all sound awfully muddled, Jane," Cathy said. "I don't think Mr. Styles knows what you mean."

"Of course he does," Jane said impatiently. "He understands perfectly well, and I think it's silly him being jealous about his brother having equal shares of the house after all this time, and he might just as well go and see his brother, and say he's sorry and then they can agree to sell the stables to Joy, and they could both help with the stables because Sue and Joy will be sure to need some men about." She stopped to draw breath.

"Because once The Grange is sold you won't be able to live here any more," she pointed out. "And you ought to be near a doctor anyway because of your rheumatism."

"I was the older brother," Jim Styles muttered. "Father had no cause to leave us equal shares."

"Well, perhaps he shouldn't have done," Jane said. "But it's too late to do anything about it now, so it's no good going on being jealous about it, is it?"

"What do you know about jealousy?" Jim asked her. "A little maid like you?"

"I know plenty about it," Jane insisted. "My father has married my governess and they're going to have a baby and I didn't want the baby one bit. I hated my stepmother and the baby and it made me feel all horrible inside. I expect it was like that with your brother, wasn't it? And if you don't talk to anyone about it, it makes it worse. I've asked God to take the jealous feeling away," she admitted. "But it's still not easy—because you don't always want it taken away—not at the time.

"Well, that's that" She got up from her chair. "We shall have to go now. Thank you for the tea, Mr. Styles, and for telling us all about Rebel. Now we can get down to the job of helping her not to be afraid. And shall we give your brother a message or something?"

Old Jim Styles gnawed his lip. "I guess you can," he said at last, a little reluctantly. "I might come over and see him afore long."

"Well, don't make it too long," Jane advised him, as the girls slipped their bridles on their ponies and fastened the throat lashes, "or you might change your mind."

The girls checked their girths and mounted. Mr. Styles held open the orchard gate.

"Goodbye, Mr. Styles," they called.

"I shall look out for pigs on the way home," Jane laughed. "But at least I know what to watch for now. Thanks a lot!"

"Gosh!" Belinda said as they trotted through the deserted stable yard and down the drive.

"You *have* got a cheek, Jane. I wonder he didn't tell you to mind your own business."

"He did really," Cathy said. "Only she didn't take any notice."

"Well, someone had to tell him," Jane said. "It was so ridiculous. Do you think he will get in touch with his brother now?"

"I do hope so," Cathy said. "But we shall have to wait and see."

"Isn't it amazing about Rebel?" Belinda said. "I can't think why we never thought of pigs. There must have been pigs around each time she played up, mustn't there?"

"What about the cattle lorry?" Cathy said. "That was one of the times she was frightened."

"It probably had pigs inside," Jane said.

"And that first time when we were going on the common," Belinda said. "I know they keep pigs in that field by the lane sometimes. I've seen them there."

"And that time she threw the little girl at the Wendover riding school," Jane said thoughtfully. "I expect the cattle market was in full swing. There would have been pigs there in some of the pens for certain."

"It's so obvious when you know," Cathy said. "It's hard to see why we didn't realise it before, with the evidence just staring us in the face."

"At least I shall be ready for it next time it happens," Jane asserted. "And be expecting trouble. I may have to get Daddy to buy a couple of pigs so that we can get her used to them again.

Perhaps if we got baby ones she wouldn't be so frightened and would begin to realize that they wouldn't hurt her."

"The blacksmith was pretty cute noticing that scar," Cathy said. "We'll have to tell him what caused it next time we see him."

"Gosh I'm tired, so much has happened today," Belinda said. "Thank goodness we're nearly home." And the others agreed.

Chapter 9

A MIDNIGHT VISIT

IT was the middle of the night, about ten days after the visit to The Grange. For a moment Jane wondered what had woken her. Then she heard her father speaking to her very softly:

"Jane, it's me. Daddy. I want you to get up very quietly so that you don't wake the others and come downstairs, I've got something to show you and something to tell you."

Jane's heart thudded in her chest and she thought that it must surely be heard all over the house. She sat up and rubbed her eyes, and then scrambled out of bed and pulled on her jodhpurs and a thick sweater. She was sure that something terrible had happened or Daddy would never have come and woken her in the night like this! Belinda was breathing deeply in her bed by the window, and Cathy, who together with her mother and father was staying at the farm while Mrs. Parminter was in hospital, trailed a foot from her camp bed.

A floor-board gave an agonized creak as Jane accidently trod on it and she nearly lost her balance as she stumbled to the door. She could see the hall light shining and could hear her father getting the car out of the garage as quietly as possibly, although the noise sounded deafening in the silence of the night.

Jane tiptoed out of the front door, closing it quietly behind her. Her father was waiting just the other side of the yard with the car's engine ticking over quietly. Jane got in.

"What's the matter, Daddy, and where are we going?"

"I've just had a phone call from the hospital," Major Parminter said. "The baby has arrived."

Jane caught her breath. "Is it . . . is it . . . ?" She was almost afraid to frame the words.

"It's a boy," Major Parminter said. "And he weighed seven and a half pounds. Isn't that splendid?"

Jane's heart was beating a little more evenly but she still couldn't feel completely sure that everything was all right.

"And Mother . . . ?" she asked tentatively.

"Mother is fine," Jane's father said. "A bit tired of course, because the baby took a long time to come and it was hard work. But she is perfectly all right. She's having a sleep right now, I think."

"But where are we going?" Jane wanted to know. "It seems so funny being up in the middle of the night like this. I thought something was wrong."

"I wanted to show you a surprise," Major Parminter said. "And I wanted us to be on our own when I showed you. You can tell the others about it later."

Major Parminter had been driving the car

along the lane that led from the Farm to the town, but now he turned off down a side lane and parked in a handy gateway. Jane could see some figures moving about down at the far end of the field and a lantern bobbing about in the darkness.

Jane's father helped her over the gate and together they walked down the field to the scene of activity.

"Who's that?" a voice said sharply out of the darkness.

"It's me—Parminter," Jane's father said. "How are things going?"

"Fine." Jane now recognized their neighbour Farmer Taylor. "The foal is a colt."

"So is mine," Jane's father said with a laugh. "Born tonight. Seven and a half pounds."

"Congratulations," Farmer Taylor said, shaking Major Parminter warmly by the hand.

Jane had moved closer and could now see the pretty chestnut mare who was busily licking the very new foal that was already standing on shaky legs and searching for his breakfast. Her face lit up in sudden recognition. "I've seen the mare before, Daddy," she cried. "When I was riding with the girls near the Common. Oh, isn't her colt beautiful?"

She felt her father's arm come round her shoulders, holding her close.

"He looks a nice little fellow," Major Parminter agreed. "As much of him as we can see anyway."

"Funny he chose the same time to come as your youngster," Farmer Taylor said. "Rather caught us napping. We didn't expect him for a couple of days."

"Well, we'll not bother the mare any more," Jane's father said. "But after your phone call I thought I'd like Jane to see him as soon as possible. It's something she won't forget for a long time."

"I certainly won't," Jane said, gazing up into the quiet starlit sky as she snuggled closer to her father. "Fancy two babies being born on the same night—my baby brother and Farmer Taylor's colt." They turned and walked back to the car.

"And there's a special connection between them," her father said. "You see, Taylor has agreed to let me have the foal when it has been weaned, and I thought that you would enjoy breaking it in. I'll give you a hand if you need it, of course. And then, when your young brother is old enough to ride, your mother and I will give you the job of teaching him. Of course you won't be able to do much with the colt for a couple of years—except handle and halter-break him and things like that, so they should just be ready together."

"Oh, Daddy, what a simply splendiferous idea!" Jane said. "No one but you would have thought of it. Just wait until I tell Cathy and Belinda about it and show them the colt."

"I'm glad you're pleased," Major Parminter said. "I know it hasn't been easy for you to accept the idea of having to share Mother and me with someone else, but I thought this might help to make it easier. And always remember, Jane, that the fact that I shall love your little brother will make no difference to the way that I love you."

"I will try and remember, Daddy," Jane said. "I am getting better, I think, and most of the time I don't mind at all. What are we going to call the baby?" she said suddenly.

"The boy or the colt?" her father asked with a laugh.

"Both," Jane said. "They'll both need a name."

"We thought about 'Christopher' for the boy," Major Parminter said. "The colt will be up to you."

"I shall have to think about it," Jane said. "It's not something you can decide in a minute."

"Shall we call in at the hospital and see if they'll let us have a look at the baby?" Major Parminter suggested. "You've missed so much sleep already that a bit more won't matter."

"Oh yes, please," Jane said. "If you think they will let us."

Jane privately thought that the colt was much prettier than the baby, but of course she didn't tell her father and her stepmother that! You couldn't see much of the baby, it was wrapped up tightly in a blanket and only its rather red face and its fluff of dark hair showed.

"He'll improve with age," Jane's stepmother said, understanding what Jane was thinking.

"He's very nice," Jane said politely. "It's just that you can't see much of him, and he's a bit small."

"He'll grow," Major Parminter assured her. "You'll be surprised how quickly he'll grow."

"Does Mother know about the colt?" Jane asked.

"Yes," Mrs. Parminter said. "And I'm so pleased he decided to come tonight. It made it extra special somehow."

"I don't know much about breaking," Jane said doubtfully.

"And I don't know much about looking after small babies," Jane's stepmother admitted. "So we'll have to learn together."

"We'd better go now," Major Parminter said. "I've got to smuggle this young lady back to bed without Cathy and Belinda knowing."

"They'll have a fit if they wake up and I'm not there!" Jane chuckled.

Jane didn't sleep much more that night, and she was very eager for Belinda and Cathy to wake up in the morning because she was just bursting to tell them her two important items of news!

Most people didn't notice the few lines in the births column of the local paper next day. *To Major and Mrs. J. Parminter of Monks Coombe, Bedborough*, it read, *a Son, Christopher*. They were too busy studying the headlines that the paper carried.

ALTERNATIVE MOTORWAY SCHEME ADOPTED.
BEDBOROUGH REPRIEVED AT THE ELEVENTH HOUR!

Jane, Belinda and Cathy heard the newspaper man shouting the news before they saw the words splashed across his newsboard. They were on their way to collect the ponies from the Styles stables after school.

"Gosh!" Belinda said. "That must mean that the stables will be safe. They won't be running the new road through Mr. Styles's property after all."

"Thank goodness for that," Cathy said. "I should have hated to see it pulled down."

"And perhaps Joy will be able to buy it now"— Jane was always practical.

"I hadn't thought about that," Cathy said. "I wonder if she will."

"I'm glad the vision didn't tarry too long," Belinda said. "I was getting tired of waiting."

"Do you think Joy *will* buy the stables?" Jane asked the others.

"There's still the other Mr. Styles to think about," Cathy reminded them. "I know he's been over to see his brother, but that doesn't mean that he'll definitely agree to sell. They might decide to stay there together."

"But they couldn't do that!" Jane protested. "Not after Joy having that message direct from God about waiting for the vision, and us happening to meet Mr. Styles's brother, and them making up the quarrel and the other motorway scheme being adopted and everything."

"There's a lot to be thought of," Cathy said sensibly. "Buying the stables is only the beginning. Running it as a Christian Riding Centre is a very big thing. There's the cooking for one thing. People who stayed at the Centre would want proper meals. If Miss Bright is in charge of the horses and Joy is in charge of the Christian Teaching side of the holiday, who is going to do the cooking?"

"What about your mother?" Jane suggested. "She's a super cook. Just look at the meals she has been making for us while my stepmother is in hospital. I bet she'd be jolly good at cooking for the Riding Centre if Joy only asked her."

"You do like to arrange things for everybody, don't you?" Belinda said with reluctant admiration.

"Well, someone's got to," Jane said.

"And what about all the tack-cleaning and mucking out and arranging for the horses to be shod and clipped and all that," Cathy said. "Who is going to do that?"

"Mr. Styles and his brother," Jane said promptly. "I think it would be a good idea if they swapped houses with Miss Bright and Joy—the cottage would be plenty big enough for them and they'd be nice and handy."

"It would be a good idea," Belinda admitted. "If they'd only agree."

By this time the three girls had reached the

stables. Mr. Styles was cleaning tack in the new tack room and he had the three ponies ready saddled and bridled for the girls.

"Have you heard the news, Mr. Styles?" Jane called.

"What news, Miss Jane?" Mr. Styles asked.

"About the new motorway! They're not coming through here after all. The Stables will be safe."

Mr. Styles beamed. "That's a good thing, then," he said. "I didn't like the idea of the old place having to go."

"How's your brother?" Belinda asked.

"Fair to middling," Mr. Styles said. "He's coming over to stay with me at the week-end. That is, if his rheumatism doesn't play him up."

"Wasn't it funny us meeting him, like that?" Jane said.

"How's that pony of yours coming on?" Mr. Styles asked. "He was telling me about her."

"Well, I've persuaded Daddy to buy a couple of piglets," Jane said. "When they get a bit bigger we're going to turn them out in the same field as Rebel and see what happens. At the moment I'm just getting her used to hearing them snuffling around the sty and making her take a look at them over the top of the pen. She's still very jumpy, but I think she's a bit better."

"Let's call in and see Miss Bright and Joy before we go home," Jane suggested to the others as they turned out of the stable yard. "I only had time

8

today to tell them about the baby coming. I haven't told them about the colt."

She banged on the cottage door.

"Bring the ponies round the back and come and have a cup of tea," Miss Bright said when she opened it. "We've just made a pot and I've got some cookies left from a batch I made last night."

"Have you seen the headlines in *The Echo*?" Joy said, waving a paper as they all came into the little sitting-room.

"Yes," Jane said. "We've been talking to Mr. Styles about it. He seems ever so pleased."

"Will you think about buying the stables now, Joy?" Cathy asked. "Do you think this is why God told you to wait, because He'd got this planned all the time?"

"I think it may be the reason, Cathy," Joy said. "Miss Bright and I were talking about it just before you came in."

"I wanted to tell you about the colt," Jane said. "Daddy got me out of bed in the middle of the night to show me Farmer Taylor's new foal. Daddy is going to buy it from him and I'm going to break it in for the baby—when they both get big enough."

"How terribly exciting," Miss Bright said. "I hope you'll let me help."

"I don't know much about it," Jane admitted. "I shall have to read lots of books and pick up all the hints I can."

"There was something I wanted to tell you

too," Joy said. "Mary and Penelope came to see me today. They wanted to know about the Bible Class."

"What about it?" Belinda said.

"They wanted to know where it was held and what time and things like that," Joy said. "They're thinking of coming."

"What, Mary and Penelope?" Jane said incredulously. "You must be joking."

"I'm not joking," Joy said. "They said you'd all been so friendly lately and so nice about lending them your ponies and teaching them to ride, they thought they'd like to come along to Bible Class and see if they could find out more about how to become a Christian. They said if it made you three change so much perhaps it could help them to change as well."

"Well I never!" Jane said. And for once she couldn't think of anything else to say.

"But we still find it hard," Belinda said. "We don't always like them, and we're not always nice."

"But you must be doing quite well," Miss Bright said. "Or they wouldn't have noticed it."

"I'm longing to see the baby, Jane," Joy said. "How long will it be before your mother is out of hospital?"

"She'll be there about ten days," Jane said. "Cathy's Mum and Dad are going to stay at the farm and look after things while she's away."

"And when she comes back they're staying on a

few days to help Mrs. Parminter," Cathy said. "So I shall be at the farm for two more weeks."

"I expect you like that," Miss Bright said. "It must make you feel like sisters, all living together under one roof."

"Mr. Styles's brother has been to see him again," Jane said suddenly. "He told us about it tonight. He's coming over to stay with him for the week-end."

"That's good," Joy said. "It looks as if you did the right thing when you told him off about the quarrel."

"I don't know how she dared!" Belinda said. "I wouldn't have done."

Joy laughed. "God uses all kinds of people in His work," she said. "Some people who are not afraid to speak out and say what is in their minds, and some people who are extra specially careful not to hurt people's feelings."

"And some people who have a lot of money left to them, and some people who have a riding stable that is too big for them that they're wanting to sell," Jane went on.

"And some people who want to be sure they're doing the thing that God wants them to, and some people who are in an awful hurry to get cracking and never mind the consequences," Joy continued with a laugh. "I'll go ahead as soon as I'm sure of the right way, Jane. Don't you worry about that. And it certainly seems that things are falling into place so quickly that I'm nearly convinced that opening a Christian Riding

Centre is what God really wants me to do with the money."

"I do hope you know soon," Jane said. "I hate waiting."

Chapter 10

A TIDY ENDING

"THERE'S going to be a gymkhana on 18th July," Jane announced to the other two girls at breakfast one morning.

Mrs. Parminter had been home from hospital with baby Christopher for two weeks but Cathy's mother still did most of the cooking at the farm, although Cathy knew they would be moving back home in a few days' time. In the meantime she was still enjoying the family feeling of living at Monks Coombe.

"Where is it going to be held?" Belinda asked. "I'm glad it's before I go to Hong Kong."

"In Bedborough," Jane said. "On the Fairfield. It's not a very big one, so the competition shouldn't be too keen."

"I shall enter Kelpie for the Potato Race, and the Bending, and the Musical Chairs," Cathy said. "He's always at his best in things that need nippiness rather than real speed."

"I've been thinking," Jane said; and then she stopped.

"What have you been thinking?" Belinda asked obligingly.

"About the girls at school," Jane said. "The ones we've been teaching to ride."

"I think they've got on jolly well," Cathy said. "Especially Sally and Joan. And even Mary and Penelope have improved enormously."

"That's what I've been thinking," Jane said.

"I do wish you'd talk sense," Belinda said. "When you've got something on your mind you always expect everyone to know all about it even without being told."

"Well," said Jane, "I've been thinking that perhaps we ought to let them go in for some of the gymkhana events instead of us."

"Oh," Belinda said. "I see."

"We could still go in for the jumping and things like that," Jane said. "But we could let them enter for some of the easier ones."

Cathy fidgeted. She hadn't owned a pony for as long as the others, and she still got a tremendous thrill from winning rosettes and seeing them flutter gaily on Kelpie's bridle.

"Do you think they'll be good enough?" she asked doubtfully.

"Well, you don't have to be madly *good*," Jane pointed out. "The Musical Chairs for instance— well, it's only a case of getting on and off and making for the nearest sack. Even Mary could do it on her head."

"She probably will," Belinda said with a giggle. "Especially if Candy moves when she's trying to mount!"

"Well, what do you think about it?" Jane demanded.

"I think it's a good idea," Belinda said, "Especially as it's only a small show. It will be a good start for them."

"And you?" Jane asked Cathy.

"Yes," Cathy said, after a short pause. "I think it's a good idea too."

"I should jolly well think so," Jane said. "Considering it was your suggestion that we ought to share the ponies in the first place, and it was you who let us in for the Saturday morning classes as well, I seem to remember."

"It has been fun though," Belinda insisted. "More than I thought it would be at first."

"And I must say the girls have been good about helping with the ponies," Jane admitted. "Even the mucking out—which isn't everyone's idea of how to spend a nice Saturday afternoon."

"Rebel's improved with the pigs, hasn't she?" Cathy said. "It was a good idea to put them in that pen and ride the ponies round and round them, getting nearer all the time."

"It's the only way to do it," Jane said. "We've got to get her so used to them that in the end she just accepts them as easily as she does a dog or a sheep.

"By the way, I showed her our baby the other day," she went on. "She didn't know what to make of him. She stretched out her neck and sniffed at him gingerly, and when he sneezed she jumped back a mile as if he was going to eat her or something."

"I think he's lovely," Cathy said. "You are

lucky, Jane. I wish we'd got a baby. I'm going to miss him when we go home."

"Well, perhaps you'll have one one day," Jane said, secretly pleased at Cathy's envy. "Although of course they're not always as nice-looking as ours," she pointed out, in a rather superior way. "Nor as good."

"You've really got quite fond of him, haven't you?" Belinda said wonderingly. "And yet only a few months ago, you were being absolutely horrible about him coming, and saying that you weren't the slightest bit interested."

Jane coloured and tossed her head. "Well, we can all change our minds, can't we?" she said.

They cantered along the grass verges on the way to school and Candy, Rebel and Kelpie sniffed the air with enjoyment, as if they were glad to be out.

Mr. Styles was waiting to take the ponies from them as Jane cleverly edged Rebel round to open the yard gate.

"Lovely morning, young misses," he greeted them.

"Yes, isn't it gorgeous," Jane said. "But it's a pity we've got to be stuck in school all day."

"Still we've got swimming this afternoon," Cathy reminded her.

"I reckon I'll turn the ponies out in the meadow for a bit," Bill Styles said. "And I'll bring 'em in later when the flies start worriting."

"Have you seen your brother lately?" Jane said, sticking her head over the half-door of the loose box where the girls were peeling off their jodhpurs and putting on their school dresses all at the same time.

"Yes I have," the stable owner answered, "and I reckon your young misses at the school may have some news for you today." Mr. Styles closed one eye and screwed up his face mysteriously.

"Have you heard something about the stables?" Jane asked in excitement.

"Jane, we'll have to go," Belinda said, giving a horrified glance at her watch. "It's gone ten to nine. We shall be late for sure."

"Oh! Botheration!" Jane said. "Well, I'm jolly well going to grab Joy at the first opportunity and if she doesn't tell me what's happening—well—I shall scream the place down."

"That should be interesting," Cathy remarked mildly. "But it will probably be Joy who will scream the place down if we're late for the first lesson—R.I.," she reminded the others.

It wasn't until lunch-time that Jane managed to corner Joy in order to question her about the hint that Bill Styles had dropped. The others helped her to hem Joy in.

"Is it settled about the stables?" Jane hissed, not very respectfully, in a stage whisper. "Mr. Styles said you might have some news for us—and we've been dying to know."

Joy shifted her pile of books to her other arm and smiled down at the three eager faces.

"Well, I can't have you dying all over the place," she said with pretended concern. "So I'd better put you out of your misery. Yes, it's settled. Miss Bright and I are taking over the stables in the autumn and Mr. Styles and his brother Jim are buying our cottage and will help Miss Bright and me with the heavier work of the stables in their spare time."

"Just as I said," Jane remarked with satisfaction. "And we'll be able to help, won't we?" she pressed.

"Oh yes," Joy said, "I'm sure we'll always be able to use another pair of hands for mucking out!"

"Oh don't be mean, Joy—Miss Wills, I mean," Jane said, remembering where she was. "I want to help you buy the horses, and the tack, and plan out the rides, and saddle up and things like that."

"I'm sure there will be plenty for everyone to do," Joy laughed. "And we definitely couldn't get anywhere without your valuable advice, Jane. And now you'll have to let me go," she insisted, "or 4S will be moaning at me for not having marked their books."

"Isn't that absolutely super?" Jane said, with a sigh of satisfaction as they walked out to the playing fields. "I do like things to work out so that everyone's happy, don't you?"

"You mean you like things to work out the way you've planned," Belinda corrected her mischievously.

"Well, I'm quite good at planning really," Jane insisted. "You must admit that."

"And so modest about it too," Cathy suggested sweetly, with a wink at Belinda.

"It's really been a very satisfactory summer," Jane said, stretching out full-length on her tummy on the new-mown grass and chewing a stalk thoughtfully. "We've found out about Belle being Rebel and why she got her name and we're more than half way to curing her of her fright."

"And Joy's decided to spend her money on a Riding Centre," Belinda put in. "I'm so glad God wanted her to use it in such an exciting way.

"And Jane's got a new brother and has learned not to be jealous of him," she added.

"Most of the time," Jane said honestly. "But sometimes I still don't want to fight against it and I just won't ask God to help me."

"It's funny," Cathy said, "how we've had to make Rebel face up to her fear so that we can help her to overcome it."

"What's so funny about that?"

"Well . . ." Cathy said. "It was the same with you and Christopher in a way. When you faced up to being jealous of the baby you got better at overcoming it too."

"I suppose I did," Jane agreed. "But I've got God to help me and poor Rebel hasn't."

"And Bill Styles has made up his quarrel with his brother Jim," Cathy went on. "And they are going to live in Joy's and Miss Bright's cottage where they will still have a job to do, but won't be overworked. Wasn't it amazing the way God worked that out?"

"And we found a way of sharing our ponies and got at least two new girls to Bible Class, and are going to let our pupils ride our ponies in some of the events in the gymkhana. I never thought that sharing our ponies would lead to that," Jane added virtuously. "And don't forget Christopher's colt— we shall soon have to start work on him," she finished.

"There's one thing you haven't quite arranged," Cathy said suddenly. "About Mummy doing the cooking for the Riding Centre."

"Well I can't do *everything*," Jane said indignantly. "They've got to learn to think of some things for themselves, after all."

"I do hope the girls do well in the gymkhana," Belinda said. "I feel responsible somehow, considering it's us who have taught them to ride."

"Well, we'll practise for the next fortnight, like mad," Jane said. "And then it will really be up to them!"

The girls were true to their word and the meadow up at Monks Coombe was the scene of constant activity for the next two weeks. Jane's voice grew quite husky with shouting at everyone, and they nearly wore out the motor of the old turn-the-handle gramophone which Jane had dug out from the attic to provide impromptu music for the Musical Chairs practices.

Mary Witter grew quite adept at tumbling on and off Candy's back at top speed, and Kelpie learned to come to a dead stop without being told, as soon as the music was stopped.

"You *must* aim carefully when you drop the potatoes in the buckets," Jane scolded Penelope for the tenth time, as they practised the potato race. "Otherwise it will take you a million years to get off and on your pony in order to pick them up, and it wastes an enormous amount of time.

"And hold the potato in your mouth when you've collected a new one," she advised Sally. "It leaves you both hands free for getting on again."

"Try to swing your body with the pony's movements in the bending race, Joan," Belinda put in. "Then it doesn't slow her down."

The girls all listened intently, and nodded obediently at their trainers' last-minute instructions.

"And make sure you're at Fairfield at least an hour before the gymkhana starts," Jane warned. "So that we have plenty of time to get you all entered for the events."

"And be sure to dress as tidily as possible," Cathy told them, "with clean shoes and fresh shirts and ties."

"And we'll lend you our hats," Belinda said. "We can swap them round according to who is riding."

Jane was at her bossiest best on the day of the gymkhana. She had got Mary into a fine state of nerves long before the time came to mount her for the Musical Chairs.

"Now don't forget!" she commanded as she checked Candy's girth. "Slip both feet out of the stirrups the moment the music stops and run *with* Candy to a sack, don't try and drag her along at the end of her reins—otherwise she'll just dig in her heels and refuse to budge an inch!"

"I'll try, Jane," Mary promised. "But I'm sure I'll never remember to do everything right."

"Don't let Jane scare you," Belinda said soothingly as she helped Joan to mount Rebel. "After all, it's only the Musical Chairs event at our own local gymkhana, and not the Show Jumping Class in the Olympic Games."

"That's not the right attitude," Jane said disapprovingly. "She's never going to get anywhere unless she takes things seriously."

Jane, Belinda and Cathy shouted themselves hoarse at the ring-side, and when Mary triumphantly won a Third rosette in the Musical Chairs their delight knew no bounds. After that even the fact that Jane and Belinda tied for first place in the Junior Jumping, and Cathy won a Second in the ponies under 14 hands class, came as an anticlimax.

"We've really done very well," Jane said when the Gymkhana was over.

"Three Thirds, four Seconds and two joint Firsts," Belinda said. "We'll pin all the rosettes up in the stable— they're going to make a smashing show."

"I can't believe I've won a rosette," Sally said with a sigh of pure happiness.

"Nor me," Joan agreed.

"And don't forget me coming third in the potato race," Penelope reminded everyone proudly. "Even though Kelpie nearly did it on his own."

"It was sporty of you to teach us to ride," Mary said.

Cathy, Belinda and Jane didn't say anything but they felt very pleased.

"It's funny," Jane said later as they were sitting at the kitchen table drinking milk and munching biscuits before they went to bed. "I would never have believed that I would feel more pleased that old Mary got a Third in the Musical Chairs than about winning a First myself in the Junior Jumping."

"Nor would I," Belinda admitted.

"It just shows," Cathy said contentedly; and the others seemed to understand what she meant without her having to go on and explain.